Mom turned her head, as if she'd known I was looking, as if I'd called her name. She turned. She waved. Not like she was saying good-bye, but like she was saying, *Hello, it's me again.*

Mom walked toward me, and now she wasn't alone. Her eyes followed a huge silver-gray dog playing around her. His head was as high as her waist, and she rested her hand on his silver-gray shoulders.

And when I looked around to see where Mom had gone, the enormous dog came running right up close to me and I saw into his soft brown eyes. His ears were up and his curved tail swayed and he looked straight at me, like he was saying, *It's you! I want to be with you!*

ALSO BY SARAH LEAN

A Hundred Horses

A Dog Called Homeless

SARAH LEAN

KATHERINE TEGEN BOOKS
An Imprint of HarperCollins Publishers

Katherine Tegen Books is an imprint of
HarperCollins Publishers.

Library of Congress Cataloging-in-Publication Data
Lean, Sarah.
A dog called Homeless / Sarah Lean. — 1st ed.
  p. cm.
Summary: Fifth grader Cally Louise Fisher stops talking, partly
because her father and brother never speak of her mother, who
died a year earlier, but visions of her mother, friendships with a
homeless man and a disabled boy, and a huge dog ensure that she
still communicates.
ISBN 978-0-06-212226-1
[1. Selective mutism—Fiction. 2. Grief—Fiction. 3. Dogs—Fiction.
4. Hearing impaired—Fiction. 5. Blind—Fiction. 6. People with
disabilities—Fiction. 7. Single-parent families—Fiction.] I. Title.
PZ7.L46333Dog 2012   2011044628
[Fic]—dc23   CIP
                                                              AC

Typography by Erin Fitzsimmons
17 18 19   BRR   10 9 8 7
❖
First paperback edition, 2014

For Dad

Without family and friends I would not have written this book. And without teachers I could not have learned how to write it. There have been many teachers, even though they may not consider themselves as such. But my thanks go especially to Derek Chorley, Chris Surtees, Roy Watson, Nick Joseph, and Julia Churchill.

And thank you all at HarperCollins for loving Homeless.

My name is Cally Louise Fisher, and I haven't spoken for thirty-one days. Talking doesn't always make things happen, however much you want it to. Think of rain; it just happens when it happens. When the clouds are ready, when they're full, they drop the water. It's not magic; it's just putting something back where it belongs.

And this is how it all began.

ᴖᴖ One ᴖᴖ

Dad's birthday, and I got up before anyone. He just wanted a quiet day. No presents, no cake, no nothing; it just wouldn't be right, he said. People forget birthdays aren't just about them.

Last year Dad's birthday was the day Mom died. I think it's called a tragedy or a catastrophe or some other big word that means more than just "bad luck" when two things like that happen on the same day.

I sat outside Dad's bedroom door with his birthday cards, waiting. Through the gap in the doorway I could just make out the dark hump under the covers and his dark head making a deep dent in his pillow. He sighed, so I knew he was awake.

There were six birthday cards for Dad: one from me, one from my older brother, Luke (still in bed or on his computer—the door was shut), and four that had come in the post. I nudged Dad's bedroom door open a bit wider and flung my card in. I saw Dad patting around the bed, feeling for the blue envelope that had landed by his back, and heard it crunch as he opened it. It was a picture of a gray bear with a blue nose. It was speaking on the telephone, and on the front it said A MESSAGE FROM ME TO YOU.

Dad said, "Thanks, that's nice."

And I said, "Are you thinking about Mom?"

Silence.

And then he said, "Get me a cup of coffee, will you?"

It didn't feel like a birthday at all, not even with the cards on top of the TV. Dad had the volume turned low while we sat around waiting for the rest of our family to arrive and come with us to visit Mom's grave for her anniversary.

ᦇ Two ᦇ

Grandpa and Grandma Hamblin picked us up and drove slowly to the cemetery. We met Granddad Fisher and Auntie Sue and walked together along paths of tidy grass and loving memories.

We made a circle, stood still as statues, not talking about her because Dad says it's too hard to talk about her. We stared at the cold gray stone marked with her name. Louise Fisher. The same as my middle name.

I thought about her, up there, somewhere. Not here. And because she was so far away, I missed her like crazy, and I wondered if I should have had some breakfast because my belly hurt so bad.

And then there she was. I saw my mom. And I know what you're thinking: you can't really see dead people. But I did. She was standing on the wall of the cemetery, wearing her red raincoat and green rain hat. And I wasn't scared. Why would I be scared of my own mom?

She put her arms out to balance, swaying as she walked along the wall. Just like she always was, doing something that made you want to laugh or do it too. She wobbled along, until she was as close as she could get to us without jumping down. She pushed her hat flat on her head. She looked at me and smiled, just like she had when she saw me sing in the school musical of *Charlotte's Web*. It made me feel special.

Grandma had a bunch of flowers wrapped in silver foil. "Be a good girl and put the flowers in the vase," she said, holding them out. Her tissue fell out of her sleeve and floated to the ground.

"Do you believe in ghosts?" I whispered, picking up her tissue and handing it back. "Do you believe Mom could come back and we could see her?"

The purple and pink flowers were reflected in

her glasses and made them look like a church window. She closed her eyes and dabbed her nose.

"Oh, dear," she said, "we're all a little upset."

She sniffed the flowers and put them in my hand.

I made my way around the tight circle of bodies and squeezed between Auntie Sue and Dad.

"Do you believe in ghosts, Auntie Sue?" I said. "Have you ever seen Mom, even though she's not supposed to be there?"

I led her arm so that she would turn around and look over at the wall, so she could see Mom, colorful and bright and real as anything. I watched her eyes for the sudden surprise. Her mouth made the shape of a smile, but she frowned. I didn't know what that meant.

"She's there, Auntie Sue," I whispered, pointing. "Over there."

She blinked. Nothing.

"Dad," I said, "look! Look over there on the wall. It's Mom!"

He rubbed his beard. They both looked at me, in that way people do when they're not really listening to what you're saying. So did Grandma and

Grandpa Hamblin and Granddad Fisher.

Granddad Fisher said, "Now, now, Cally, it's nei-ther the time nor place for silly games."

Then Grandpa Hamblin looked at the sky, at the distant gray clouds. "Rain's on its way," he muttered.

Dad looked at the silent earth.

"Dad," I said, "I can see her. I know she's dead, but she's here."

And right then, when I looked across and Mom's eyes shone as bright as a whole sky full of sunshine, I felt that her and me were the only ones truly alive. My heart thumped, my lungs filled, and I wanted to shout, "Mom, sing a song; then they'll hear you. Make the birds wonder, just like you used to."

"Cally, love," Auntie Sue said, "sometimes our imaginations play tricks on us." She reached around and rested her hand on Dad's shoulder. "Sometimes, when you really want to believe something, you can make it seem true."

Tears smudged her mascara. Grandma blew into her tissue.

I thought I heard something, like when the car-nival starts and you're miles away at the other end of town but you know it's coming. Mom made a funnel of her hands, like a loudspeaker.

"Dad, she wants to tell us something," I said.

I saw into his eyes before he looked away, as if all the words waiting there were too big to pronounce, too hard to say properly. He hunched his shoulders, rubbed his face.

"Enough, Cally," he said, "you're upsetting people."

I whispered, "Can't you see her?"

She'd stopped smiling. She searched her pocket as if she were trying to find something. I wondered why she had a coat and hat on when it was such a warm spring day.

"Dad"—I pointed—"you can see her, can't you?"

"No," he growled, "and neither can you. And I don't want to hear another word about it."

❧ Three ❧

"**G**et into groups of two or three. Each group will represent a planet," said Miss Steadman in science. "As it's stopped raining, we're going out to the playground to map out the solar system."

I said to Mia Johnson, who was my best friend, "Let's us two be Earth."

Then Daisy Bouvier came over, chewing her nails. She hung around us like she'd been doing a lot lately since she had a fight with Florence Green at a sleepover. Mia looked at me funny and said, "Daisy, you're in my group too."

Miss Steadman started talking about planets

being millions of miles away and that we had to pretend the playground was the whole solar system. I nudged Mia and tried to whisper about what us two could do at break time, not including Daisy. But I couldn't tell her because Miss Steadman said, "Shush, Cally. Let's try very hard today to not talk when I'm speaking. Otherwise you won't learn anything."

She marked our place with a blue chalk circle and set off to Mars, another group, with some red chalk.

Being in the solar system reminded me of the day when our family had gone to visit a big old cathedral. Inside the enormous yellow cathedral was one of the oldest clocks in the world. The earth was painted in the middle of the clock, and the ancient sun circled around the outside on the long hand.

Mom had said, "Sometimes people get things the wrong way around."

Because it was made hundreds of years ago, the people who painted it didn't know what the universe was like. Now everyone knows we are the ones spinning on our tiny planet through space, circling the sun. It's funny how that happens and we can't even feel it.

"Look," I said to Mia and Daisy, "this is how our planet spins."

With my arms out I went around and around. It made my hands go heavy and my eyes go giddy.

"Stop it," said Mia. "We're supposed to be listening, not talking and spinning."

"You could be the moon," I said to Daisy.

"Miss Steadman didn't say to be a moon," she said. "And I wanted to be Mercury."

"But look," I said, "look what would happen if we suddenly started spinning a different way."

I bumped into the moon, and that made me fly off in a different direction.

"Look," I said, "we could go right out into space and see what's there."

"Cally Fisher!" Miss Steadman shouted across the galaxy. "Go back to your circle and stay there!"

But I wanted to see what was out there. I imagined a splash of light winking from across the universe. Maybe it was a star; maybe it was a doorway, a way through a hole in the sky where souls and angels go. And who wouldn't want to find out what was shining in the darkness when it's the only bright thing in the whole of space?

Anyway, I got sent to Pluto with Daniel Bird, who didn't have a partner.

"You're in trouble again," he said, because he is always stating the obvious.

ᏃᎨᏩ*Four*ᏃᎨᏩ

We had music next with Mr. Crisp. I love singing. I get that from my mom. She would sing, and Dad would say the early-morning birds ought to think about getting another job. Mom said singing is like knitting; it ties everything together, especially people. That's why Dad played the guitar for her and why he played in a band down at the pub on Friday nights. Well, he used to.

So when Mr. Crisp said we were doing a farewell concert at the end of the term, me and Mia said we'd put our names down for the auditions to sing together, seeing as it was our last year at Parkside Juniors.

Then, after music, I heard Daisy talking to Mia in the girls' room.

Daisy said, "Let's just put our names down to do something on our own. We'll just not tell her."

Mia said, "We could do a duet, seeing as we're best friends now."

They talked about some songs they liked.

"She'd only drown us out anyway," said Daisy.

They laughed, and Mia said, "Actually, I think she's a rubbish singer."

Then they came around the corner of the stalls, and Mia slammed, *smack!* right into me in the door-way.

"I'm not rubbish," I said.

Her eyes flashed. "I never said that."

"I heard you."

Mia went red. She punched her hands on her hips.

"I was only joking," she said.

"She can't take a joke," said Daisy.

"And anyway, every time we do something with

you, you always get in trouble. And you always make such a big fuss about everything."

"No, I don't," I said.

"Yes, you do!" said Mia.

"No, I don't! And you're supposed to be my friend."

"See, you're doing it now. You just spoil everything. And I never said for definite I was going to do it with you."

"You're not a very good friend. Good friends wouldn't say things like that."

"Well, if that's how you feel," said Mia, hooking Daisy's arm and marching down the corridor, "we don't have to be friends anymore."

I stayed in the bathroom stall with the door locked, peeling bits of plastic off the scabby patch by the toilet paper dispenser until the bell rang.

I could still put my name down for the concert. Only now I'd have to sing on my own.

❧ *Five* ❧

"Quiet, please. Everyone look this way. Cally . . . Cally!" Miss Steadman glared. "Put the marker down. Now, please. Thank you, Cally. Now, I have something to tell you all."

After attendance Miss Steadman told us that our school was going to raise money for a charity called Angela's Hospice. Angela's Hospice is a place nearby where they care for sick children and try and make their wishes come true. Miss Steadman said the members of the student council would be along in a minute to tell us how we were going to raise the money.

While we waited for them, Miss Steadman asked

us what our wishes were. We wished for fast cars (mostly boys), to meet famous people, for new computers and Xboxes, that all the tigers, bears, dolphins, and whales were saved (mostly girls), and to save the planet.

"I wish I had a rocket to fly to the stars," I said.

Then Daniel Bird shouted out, "I wish I could win the lottery. Then I could buy a time machine and go back to the day I cut off half my finger when Granddad squashed it in his deck chair." Daniel held his hand up so we could all see where there was a missing bit. "Then I'd take it to the hospital in a bag of ice and they could sew it back on."

I said, "Why don't you have the time machine take you back to just before your granddad sat down and get your hand out of the way?" Obviously.

"Don't be stupid," said Daniel. "There's no such thing as time machines."

He was so annoying.

"That's enough bickering, Cally, Daniel," said Miss Steadman. "What other wishes do we have?"

Daisy said she wished for world peace. Mia folded her arms and scowled at me. I thought she'd be wishing her hair wasn't so frizzy. Instead she said, "I wish that this year's concert will be the best one ever."

Daniel continued. "I wish I could go to Disneyland, Miss."

Miss Steadman stopped the calling out, saying, "Funny Daniel should mention Disneyland, because sometimes the children at Angela's Hospice have that same wish." Her voice went quiet. "It's good to remember how lucky we are to be healthy. The money we'll raise isn't just for trips to Disneyland. It's also for expensive medical equipment for very sick children."

Just then the two children from the student council came in. Jessica Stubbs and Harry Turner were holding a piece of paper between them and stood at the front of the class.

"The student council has decided we're going to do a sponsored silence to raise money for Angela's Hospice," said Jessica, reading from the sheet. "We need three volunteers from each class to be silent, and hopefully everyone will sponsor them."

Harry waved the sponsorship forms.

I wasn't really listening. The tip of my green marker had gone inside the tube. I was trying to poke it out with a compass under the desk. We had geography next, and you always need a green marker in geography.

"We're going to do it next Tuesday," said Harry. "The people doing the silence are not allowed to talk between nine o'clock in the morning and three o'clock in the afternoon."

"You have to be really sure you can do it," said Jessica.

I took off the bottom end of the pen and poked through the top again. The inky felt shot out and landed on the floor by Florence. I tried to tell her to roll it over with her feet. She told me to shush. I told her to get it quick because it might leak into the carpet.

"It's for an important cause," said Jessica.

Miss Steadman rapped on her desk. "What's going on over there now?" she said sharply.

"Cally wasn't listening and was trying to distract me," Florence told her.

"I was just—" I started to say, but Miss Steadman interrupted.

"Enough tattling, thank you!" she snapped. "Or

we'll be having words at the end of the day again."

I watched the marker ink make a dark patch on the carpet.

"So," she continued, taking a deep breath, "who thinks they can manage to be silent for a whole school day? Any volunteers?" She scanned the room, straightaway looking at the quiet ones and the good ones. She nodded and smiled and thanked the two children who put their hands up, and their names got added to the list.

"One more volunteer?" Miss Steadman asked.

Then I saw her eyes flick across to me. They silently said, "Not you, Cally Fisher, not you. You can't do it."

I'd seen the same disappointed, disbelieving eyes look at me like that the weekend before at the cemetery. Then she looked away, just like Dad had done. Sometimes you just have to prove people wrong. Sometimes you just want someone to believe you're more than they think you are. Plus there was also the fact that the sneaky traitor Mia was about to put her hand up.

I reached over and held Mia's arm down and shot

my hand in the air. I ignored the giggles and whispers, the feet reaching out to nudge each other. I ignored Daniel Bird's loud "Ha!" and Mia's gaping mouth. Jessica and Harry looked at Miss Steadman, Jessica's pencil poised, not writing my name on their list. Miss Steadman shushed the murmurings and giggling and looked out the window. Then she looked in the grade book register as if she were checking for something. Her mouth twitched. She took a deep breath and straightened her back.

"What we need is—"

"It's for an important cause," I said quickly.

Just then I saw Daisy whispering to Mia. I saw Mia smirk and fold her arms, her eyes go narrow.

I straightened my arm, zipped my lips. Miss Steadman leaned back into her chair. I saw her heart go soft.

"What we need is people like you, Cally, who are willing to take up the challenge. Thank you, you can put your hand down now."

She nodded to Jessica as if to say, "Why aren't you writing her name down already?"

"Everyone else can be involved by sponsoring

our volunteers. You will need to ask your parents. Remember what the money is for."

She closed the grade book, kept her eyes on me.

"And our volunteers are going to need your support, not just with sponsorship money. You're all going to have to encourage them to stay quiet."

ᴖ Six ᴖ

Mrs. Brooks, the special needs lady, wanted to see me. She deals with all the problems—if you can't do math or English, if you're in a wheelchair, or if you are the problem. She's a tall lady with plum-colored hair, orangey lipstick, and an orangey tan. She looks like she's just come out of a hot pan. Her perfume made it difficult to breathe around her.

For a while after Mom died, she let me sit with her and draw pictures. She said I could talk about anything I wanted. But mostly she did the talking, mostly in riddles.

"I hear you've volunteered for the sponsored

silence," she said.

"Miss Steadman said I could."

"Yes, she did. And we'll all support you."

She ran a finger around the gold chain on her sunglasses, which she wore on her head all year, even inside school. She tilted her head and smiled.

"Well, I want you to know if for any reason you don't feel you can manage a whole day of silence, then Mia Johnson has very kindly volunteered to do the morning."

She reached out to touch my arm. I hate it when people look sorry for you. I hate it when they look at you like you're hopeless.

"Perhaps you could each do half the day?" she said.

"I can do it," I said.

"She's just being a good friend—"

"I can do it all day!"

She signed my sponsorship form and said, "If you change your mind . . . ," but she didn't finish her sentence.

She leaned back in her chair and held her sunglasses up to the light.

"I remember you in third grade," she said,

huffing on the lens. "You were a lovely little girl who used to get along with people. You worked really hard to remember all your lines and songs for *Charlotte's Web*. And I'm sure you would have been brilliant again last year. . . ."

She poked me with her orange fingernail.

"Wouldn't it be nice to have the old Cally back?"

I told you she talked in riddles. And you can't go back. There's no such thing as time machines. Ask Daniel Bird.

"I've never been old," I said.

Not like her. That wouldn't be for at least another eighty years.

"What I meant was—"

"You mean I used to be good and nice and now I'm not."

"No, of course not. What I meant was you've had some difficult challenges. Things happen in our lives that can change us, make us unsettled."

She sighed. "It was such a shame you had to pull out of the show last year. Such terrible timing."

And the reason she said that was that I was sup-posed to be playing Olivia in the musical called

Olivia!, which is just like *Oliver Twist* but with a girl. But because the show was only two days after the accident when Mom died, everyone said I shouldn't. Daisy stepped in.

Mrs. Brooks put her glasses back on her head and pulled a black file off the shelf. It said FIFTH GRADE ASSESSMENTS on the side. She flicked through the file, running her finger along pages to find my name, and tapped the page slowly.

"Perhaps it would be better to think about the future, a fresh start. I hope you're going to be singing in the farewell concert."

And on she went.

I hadn't put my name down for the concert yet. I looked past her, out through the dusty window, across the wide playing field.

And there she was. Mom came through the open gates. She walked across the grass and headed for the lunch benches at the front of the school, like she'd had some good news but didn't want to rush to tell anyone. Mom was wearing her red raincoat again and looked like the only red apple in a tree.

I stretched myself as tall as I could to see over

Mrs. Brooks's wide shoulders while she jabbered on.

"Sitting up straight is a good place to start," Mrs. Brooks said. "You look more grown up already."

I waited until she went back to the file and the jabbering, then leaned to the side to see better. I so wanted Mom to see me. And even though there was a playing field and the school walls and window between us, Mom turned her head, as if she'd known I was looking, as if I'd called her name. She turned. She waved. Not like she was saying good-bye, but like she was saying, *Hello, it's me again.*

"Did you want to ask something?" said Mrs. Brooks, seeing me with my arm in the air.

"No," I said. And then: "Can I go to the bathroom?"

Mrs. Brooks looked out the window over her shoulder. She didn't see Mom; she didn't see anyone there.

"Be quick," she said.

My heart pounded as I passed the girls' bathroom. My breathing was so loud and fast, I thought that everyone could hear me, but I didn't even look up to see if anyone in the office saw me go out the doors at reception.

Mom walked toward me, and now she wasn't alone. Her eyes followed a huge silver-gray dog playing around her. His head was as high as her waist, and she rested her hand on his silver-gray shoulders.

Mom looked at the dog, and then she looked up at me.

"Stop right there, Cally Fisher!"

Mr. Brown, the head teacher, and Mrs. Brooks were running across the playing field.

Mrs. Brooks shouted again, "Stay where you are! Don't move!"

Her sunglasses bounced off her head and fell on the grass, but she kept coming.

And when I looked around to see where Mom had gone, the enormous dog came running right up close to me and I saw into his soft brown eyes. His ears were up and his curved tail swayed and he looked straight at me, like he was saying, *It's you! I want to be with you!*

I thought, That dog's not a ghost; he's really real.

And just as Mr. Brown came closer, the dog changed direction and galloped away. He raced around Mrs. Brooks and snatched up her sunglasses and dropped them again, daring her to take them.

I could hear her saying, "Nice doggy," and, "There's a good doggy," and then, "Somebody get some more help!"

The dog's stride was so big, nobody could catch him. By the time they were all red in the face and more people from the school came out to help, the dog had jumped over the fence and run away with Mrs. Brooks's sunglasses.

Then Mrs. Brooks had my elbow and was taking me back to her office.

"I'll deal with this, Mr. Brown," she called. "What on earth did you think you were doing, Cally? I think we need to have another chat."

But there wasn't time. Daniel Bird was standing in the doorway of her office, poking bits of Silly Putty into the door catch while he waited for his session.

"What's she done now?" he asked.

I still had a picture of Mom and the dog in my mind, clear and bright and beautiful. And all I could think was that they'd both come to me, without my even asking.

❧ Seven ❧

I took the sponsorship form home. Luke signed it. My brother's thirteen. He looks like my mom: he's got her thick brown hair, and he's just about as tall as she was. But he's serious and boring.

I get on Luke's nerves. I have to. He spends a lot of time in his room by himself, racing cars on his computer. His ambition is to beat someone called Sting who has the highest score. He tells me to shut up all the time; he can't break records and reduce his lap times with me banging about in the background. Dad tells me to leave him alone. He says you have to give a man a bit of peace and quiet. I remember Mom used to say she liked noise in the house. She said, "When the kids are quiet, you know there's trouble." But Dad doesn't seem to remember anything she used to say.

Luke calculated sponsoring me probably wouldn't cost him much. But he said it would be worth every penny. "I wish it were forever," he said.

"Be careful what you wish for"—that's what Mom would have said.

"Dad, guess what?" Luke said, flinging the form miles away from my hands. "I've taken one point four seconds off my lap time." He slid over the back of the sofa and sat next to Dad, slumping his feet on the table.

"Hmm?" said Dad.

"And that was in heavy rain."

"Good for you," Dad said, without looking away from the TV. "Take your feet off the table. And sit down, Cally. I'm trying to watch this."

When the detective show finished, I showed Dad the sponsorship form. He read the details.

"Sponsored silence, eh?"

"Miss Steadman said I could do it."

"She did?"

"And Mrs. Brooks."

"Good old Mrs. Brooks," he muttered. Which isn't what he usually said about her. "Next Tuesday?"

"All day. Why?"

"Nothing. There's a meeting at work—I'm going to be home late, that's all."

He wrote "fifty cents" in the box on the form that said how much you were going to pledge for each hour of silence. Then he looked at the TV again.

"Dad," I said, "I saw Mom again. She came to school."

He closed his eyes and rubbed his eyebrows, shook his head.

"She brought a dog with her."

Dad crossed out the "fifty cents" and changed it to "one dollar." "Time for bed," he said.

I watched him flick the channels to find another detective show. He liked mysteries; he liked to try to guess who done it.

❧ Eight ❧

At seven o'clock on Tuesday morning I lay in bed thinking about my mom and the giant silver-gray dog. In my daydream I said, *Mom, where are you?* and she said, *Hello, Cally, I'm right here.* And I said, "Where?" And she said, *About an inch away.*

I felt her nearness, but I couldn't see her.

I opened my eyes.

I watched the dust fairies trapped in a stream of sunlight between the curtains, little pieces of almost nothing that disappeared when the sun went in. Slowly and silently they turned, undecided about which way to go. They coasted and floated. I whispered to them because they were small and fragile. "Make up your mind," I said. Then I blew on them, and soon they were whirling away.

Dad came in. Same old checked shirt with the ink stain on the pocket, same old crumpled work trousers. Same old messy hair and beard, dark and speckled with gray, like he'd been out overnight in a frost.

"You awake?" he said.

He picked my school clothes off the floor and put them on the end of my bed. He stood there a minute.

"You've got that charity thing today, haven't you?"

"Sponsored silence," I said.

It was nice that he remembered. He was so forgetful these days. He forgot he had to do the ironing. He forgot to shave. He forgot to pay the phone bill, and it took weeks for them to connect us up again. He was just like a raggedy old bear still sleepy from hibernating over winter. Except winter was ages ago. He used to be a different sort of dad— always joking with Luke, rough-and-tumbling on the sofa. He always helped me with math homework, right after dinner. He'd show me how to do a question; then he'd do a bit, and I'd finish it, until I could do it by myself. You could sit on his lap and he'd listen to you tell him anything.

I climbed out from under the bedcovers and stood up on the bed so I was as tall as he was. I held his face in my hands, like he used to do to me. I wanted to say something about Mom, to say *remember when . . . remember?* Like I'd already asked a thousand times. I searched his eyes, looked to see if Mom was in there. But it was like the morning after there's been heaps of snow and you can't tell what's underneath anymore.

So I said, "Dad? What if I can't help it and I say something?"

He squeezed me.

"I won't mind. You'll be doing your best."

He went off in a dream, opened the curtains, sent the dust fairies into the shadows.

So that was it. My best didn't sound like much. He was just the same as all the others who didn't think I could do it.

"I'll mind," I whispered to the invisible spinning dust. And those were my final words.

❦Nine❦

I started my silence at four minutes past seven.
At half past seven when Dad said, "Cornflakes
or Rice Krispies?" I put my finger across my
lips and waited until he turned around to see why
I wasn't answering.

"Getting a bit of practice in?" he said, taking both
boxes from the shelf. "Don't forget I'm going to be
home late. There's a couple of cans of spaghetti in
the cupboard."

At eight o'clock I jangled the coins in my pocket
when he asked if I had my bus money. Luke rolled
his eyes and sighed.

After attendance the sponsored silence volunteers

were excused from answering any questions in lessons. Everyone was asked not to distract us.

By ten o'clock Miss Steadman was already looking impressed.

At break time nobody seemed to mind I wasn't playing.

At half past twelve all of us volunteers sat on the benches outside to eat our bagged lunches in silence. I could see through the tall glass doors into the assembly hall. Mr. Crisp, the music teacher, was auditioning people for the farewell concert. I saw Mia and Daisy standing on the stage together, their mouths opening and closing.

During history Mrs. Brooks came in and winked at me.

At quarter to three Miss Steadman was looking proud. She told us we were all going to a short assembly with Mr. Brown.

I'd done it. I'd proved them wrong: Miss Steadman, Mia, Daniel, and all the rest of them who didn't think I could do it. And it should have been over at three o'clock. Only I wasn't just happy that some sick children might get to go to Disneyland. The day had passed, and I'd not been in trouble, not fallen out with anyone; nobody had told me to be quiet. Nobody had said anything to me at all.

The twenty-four sponsored silence volunteers were called to the front of the assembly. Children clapped and cheered while Mr. Brown showed some pictures of happy children from the Angela's Hospice website on the screen. He praised us for meeting a difficult challenge, then said he would add up the sponsorship money when it was collected and let us know the total by the end of the following week.

"The children from Angela's Hospice will be very grateful," he said. "Your silence has helped make their wishes come true. Now you may speak."

There were big whoops from the other volunteers, coughing and gabbling like mad, saying things like "That was soooo hard" and "I almost said something when . . ."

The talking and laughing bubbled everywhere. I wanted to say something. But there was only one thing on my mind, only one person I wanted to say it to. And I could say it inside, could say it without anyone hearing: *Mom, did you find that dog in heaven?*

❧ Ten ❧

Saturday morning me, Luke, and Dad took the bus into town. Dad told us to wait outside the bank; there was something important he had to go do. He'd be about ten minutes. He looked as if he were going to say something else, but he didn't.

We leaned against the wall between the bank and Crumbs the Baker's, sniffing in the smell of hot pastries, listening to the beeps of the ATM in the wall.

"Wanna go in Game for a minute?" Luke said, nudging me.

As if.

"Suit yourself," said Luke, shrugging in his sloppy jacket. "Don't think I haven't noticed, though," he muttered. "You're up to something. I can tell."

Instead I sat on a bench and watched a man in a puffy purple jacket sitting on the sidewalk on the other side of the street. One of his old sneakers was split, and you could see his dirty sock poking out the hole. He was juggling with some balls made of wadded-up newspaper.

He had an orange woolly hat to collect money and a cardboard sign leaning against his knee, saying HUNGRY. I thought if he wrote it himself, he had quite nice writing. Better than mine anyway.

People passed him by. I suppose he lived on the streets, and so nobody noticed him. He concentrated on the balls of paper flying through his hands, and now and again he looked up when somebody passed him, making him drop the balls.

Just then a gang of boys, all a bit bigger than Luke, and even moodier-looking, stopped and leaned against the wall next to him. They looked around. They shifted their feet, stuffed their hands in their pockets, and circled the man.

The paper balls tumbled into his lap. One boy with dark wavy hair kicked the HUNGRY sign over. He laughed and grabbed the woolly hat, scooping the coins out. Coins trickled from between his fingers, bounced, and circled on the pavement.

"Leave him alone!" shouted a big lady wearing an apron, stomping out of the bakery. She waved her arms. "Go on, clear off, he's done nothing to you."

The gang looked at her, and people slowed and looked at them. The man stared at something else down the street.

"I'm calling the police!" she said, rushing back toward the shop.

The boys ran, pushing one another out of the way, making a ripple through the shoppers, shouting rude things. The orange hat got thrown down and people walked right over it.

I went and picked it up.

The man was on his knees, collecting the coins off the pavement. The baker lady from Crumbs came up to me, holding a paper bag stuffed with pastries.

"There's a good girl," she said, her voice as soft as dough. "Jed's shy, and he wouldn't harm a fly. Came into town a while ago now, looking for somebody, I think." She smiled like she was sad for him, then sighed. "Poor man. All he seems to have found is a lot of bother with those troublesome boys."

She shook her head and handed me the bag.

"Go on," she said. "You give them to Jed. I'd better be getting back to the counter."

I had to crouch down to get Jed's attention because he was busy packing all his things into shopping bags. Then he did that thing when you look away and then look back again quickly, like you didn't realize who it was or what was happening the first time. I heard him take a sharp breath.

I had my pocket money in my hand and held it out for Jed to see. I opened the hat and dropped the coins in, but he didn't look at them. I could tell he was really glad because he stared right into my eyes and smiled. His eyes were lovely, silver warm and sparkling. A rush of air came from his mouth because he had been holding his breath, and now he was so relieved and happy to have his money back.

I handed Jed the bag of food.

Then Luke was back, pulling at my arm and

saying, "What're you doing, Cally? Come on, you know what Dad thinks!"

Dad said homeless people had a choice just like everyone else. We weren't allowed to give them money. They chose to live on the streets. They'd made their own problems and had to sort them out themselves.

"You didn't buy him food as well, did you?" Luke whispered through his teeth. "Dad'll be mad!"

Jed didn't say anything; he just stood there and kept smiling. He had surprisingly white teeth. So I smiled back. It was kind of like talking but not talking. I didn't know what we were saying, but it was something nice. Then, just like that, he handed me his HUNGRY sign. His loose sole scuffed along the pavement as he walked away.

"What's the matter with you?" asked Luke, dragging me away. "Dad's coming!"

I followed his eyes and saw Dad coming down the steps of the bank, leafing through a pile of papers.

"All right, kids?" he said. "What have you been up to?"

Luke frowned and took a deep breath. "Nothing

much," he said slowly, narrowing his eyes.

"What's that you got there?" Dad said to me, rolling his papers into a tube. I held Jed's sign up to show him.

"Just what I was thinking. How about pizza then?" he said, looking over his shoulder at Pizza Palace.

But it wasn't the red tablecloths and drippy candles in the window of Pizza Palace that caught my eye. It was a red raincoat. Mom was standing by The Music Shop on the other side of Pizza Palace. She put her face close to the window and looked inside. And then, just when Jed came past her, she joined him, walked alongside him. They turned into the alleyway side by side.

❧ Eleven ❧

Dad still hadn't noticed I wasn't talking, didn't say anything when I pointed at the picture of the ham-and-mushroom pizza on the menu.

"Why did you bring us here?" said Luke, chomping tomato mush.

"You like pizza, don't you?" said Dad, not looking up.

"Yeah, but I mean we don't normally go out for pizza."

Dad wiped his mouth and hands with his napkin, took ages to answer. Eventually he said, "Just thought you needed a treat, that's all."

"Why, what's happened?"

"Can't I just take you out?" Dad snapped.

"I'm just saying!" moaned Luke. "Unlike some people."

He swung his leg under the table until it nudged my shin. I swung my foot back. I dodged him and screwed my mouth tight. We scuffled under the table, kicking each other.

"Hey! What's with you two?" Dad snapped as I hit his leg by mistake.

"It's her," said Luke. "She's being weird!"

"Cut it out, both of you!"

I didn't finish my pizza. I slid the last slice under the table, wrapped it in my napkin, and squashed it into my jeans pocket. Just in case I saw Jed again.

The waitress arrived with the bill. Dad pinned on a smile for her. His flat smile. The one that said he was trying to be cheerful.

"Dad?" Luke said as Dad took his wallet out. "You know we're not supposed to give money to people on the streets?"

I leaned back, folded my arms, silently dared him to tell.

"Well, what if you give food to one, like a muffin or some pizza, does that count?" Luke said the words *muffin* and *pizza* loudly and spit wet crumbs across the table. He can be so disgusting.

"First we've got to make sure *we've* got enough," Dad said, pulling out his wallet.

It was bulging with money. Both of us noticed. His wallet had never, ever looked like that before. I thought he'd won the lottery, but he couldn't have. We'd be buying the biggest flat-screen HDTV you've ever seen and every episode of *CSI* on DVD.

"But is it all right?" Luke pressed, still staring at the cash.

Dad wasn't looking at him. "No, it's not all right," he snapped. "I don't want you giving them money, food, or anything."

Luke swung his leg at me again.

Dad went on. "There are some people in this world who don't have much, but they still manage to feed their kids and put a roof over their heads. Even if it's a small roof."

He stood up, looked us both in the eye.

"Come on," he said. "We're going to the playground."

We'd sort of grown out of going to the playground, and if you haven't been for a long time, you feel like it doesn't belong to you anymore. You let other people have a turn on the swings even though they're not bigger than you and they've only been leaning on the bars for a minute.

I went over to the garden area where adults usually go to sit away from the noisy kids. Luke climbed a tree. Dad sat on a bench by the tree, leaning on his knees unrolling and rolling his papers. Sometimes you can be a family and not all want to sit together.

And I was just thinking about things, like how come Mom was with Jed, and did he see her too, when I heard some rustling in the bushes behind me.

The huge silver-gray dog, the same one I'd seen with Mom on the school playing field, came bounding out.

I sucked in my breath, held my arms in tight. The dog nudged my hand, pushing his nose under so I'd have to stroke him. He circled over and over. Then he sat down, his tail sweeping the gravel side to side, side to side. His head was as high as my chest; his small brown eyes sparkled like a million stars. His eyebrows and beardy chin and whiskers twitched so you could tell what his face was saying. And it was saying, *I want to be with you!*

I very, very nearly called out. Not because I was afraid but because sometimes you just can't help it. And I could feel the words bubbling up: *Look, Mom, look! Isn't he beautiful?* And it made me laugh, even though she wasn't there.

Just then I made my one and only rule for not speaking. I was allowed to laugh. Because laughing isn't words. Nobody knows what you are saying, but everyone knows what you mean. Even a dog.

❧ Twelve ❧

I'd been saving the leftover pizza for Jed, but the dog sniffed around my pocket. He took the pizza gently from the napkin and gulped it down. Then he licked my fingers. I patted him and stroked him. I couldn't help loving him.

Then Dad called, told me and Luke to come over. The dog followed without my even asking. That's the brilliant thing about dogs. They don't say, "Where are we going?" They just come with you.

Luke ducked out of the way as the dog trotted beside me toward him but was soon ruffling and patting him and looking impressed. But not Dad.

"Where on *earth* did it come from?" Dad yelled,

pulling us behind him like he was snatching us out of the mouth of a monster.

The dog hung back, his head down, his tail still.

Dad tried to find the word that would make the dog go away; he flapped his arms and said, "Shoo, go on! Fetch! Off with you! *Go away!*"

He was just like the people at school. They were scared of the dog because he was so big. They didn't stop to look into his soft eyes and see he wasn't trying to do any harm.

I kept looking around, thinking Mom might be there, somewhere.

The dog's ears went up, as if he had heard something, and he suddenly bounded off in big lolloping gallops, like he was in slow motion. He disappeared behind the bushes.

Dad turned to me, shouting, "For heaven's sake, Cally! What're you thinking?" He paced and shouted some more. "You should know better than to go up to a strange dog without checking with the owner or without checking with me first."

He looked at me. He rolled his papers. I could see he was trying really hard not to blow his top. "Don't do that again. D'you hear me?" He took a breath to calm down. "Are you all right?"

Obviously not now that he'd shouted at me.

Dad sat down hard on the bench, curling the papers into a tight tube. He looked at his watch. He muttered, "Sorry," and something about everything's going to be fine.

I could feel something bad coming with those words. Why do people say everything's going to be fine when they don't mean it at all? It's what the nurse says before she jabs you with a needle. Before she rubs alcohol on your cut and makes it sting like crazy. After she tells you she's very sorry that your mom's never coming back. They are going to hurt you and then give you something stupid like a cherry lollipop. That's how you know it's not going to be fine.

Dad took a deep breath and sat us down on either side of him. He unrolled his papers.

"I've got something to show you," he said.

He smoothed out the sheets. The top one said SECOND FLOOR APARTMENT TO RENT, OVERLOOKING THE COMMON.

He said, "We've got to move out of our house."

Nobody said anything. When you don't want to

believe something, it's like you get instantly frozen in ice. You can't move and you can't blink.

As we left the playground, Luke was saying, "What do you mean? Why are we moving? Where are we going?" Hundreds of questions.

But Dad wouldn't answer. He just said, "Don't say anything until you've seen it."

And I didn't say anything. Because I was already sure by then that nothing I said would make any difference.

But what I remember most was that was the day I decided the big silver-gray dog's name was going to be Homeless. And that was because Jed was standing on the other side of the road opposite the playground. He was wearing a big pair of sunglasses, Mrs. Brooks's sunglasses. Next to him was the giant silver-gray dog with a cardboard sign around his neck. It said HOMELESS.

❧ Thirteen ❧

Four Albert Terrace was a tall house made of rust-colored bricks, with crumbly gray cement in between. The blue paint flaked around the big windows made it look as if it had sad old eyes. Our house had just been built when Mom and Dad moved in. Everything in it was ours. The builders made the outside; Mom made the inside. She varnished the window frames every year, to keep them shiny.

A car pulled up, and a lanky man got out. He buttoned his gray jacket and said, "Hello, kiddi-winks," but Dad didn't make us say hello back.

He handed Dad a key, held his arm out, and said,

"It's got great views over the common and good-sized bedrooms; it's a fine example of Victorian history."

We've done Victorian history at school, and I learned what it was like for children living back then when we rehearsed for *Olivia!*: misery, disease, and empty bellies.

The small garden at the front had a pot of sunflowers with green heads tethered to sticks; there was a small concrete yard out the back. We were going to have to share the garden and yard and a clothesline and a shed with the people in the apartment downstairs.

The second-floor apartment was empty. Our footsteps were loud along the hall and in the hollow rooms. The rooms were all painted the same plain color, like old book pages; they smelled of dust and other people.

We all looked out the window at the common, a big patch of land for everyone.

Dad nodded toward the view.

"Somewhere for you to throw a Frisbee, hey, Luke?"

Luke went out, slamming the door. The bang crashed into the walls of the empty rooms. Through the window I saw Luke running across the common. Dad swore. I said my twelve times table in my head. Miss Steadman said I needed more practice, and you can't remember your tables unless you keep saying them over and over and over.

The lanky man was still waiting outside.

"I'm sure you're going to like it here," he said. But I could tell he didn't care because he was staring at the big wad of money in Dad's wallet. They signed bits of paper and swapped them.

We found Luke throwing stones into the stream under a little brick bridge. His face was blotchy.

"I'm sorry, son," said Dad, "but we don't have a choice."

"This is your choice, not ours," said Luke, spitting out the words.

Luke looked at me, knew I was with him. We would never choose to leave our home. Mom was still in every cupboard Dad had made for her, along every shelf he had put up and she had painted. She was in the soft carpets and the flowery paper on their bedroom wall, in the light switches, on every handle of every door she'd held open, in the grain of the wooden kitchen table where she'd always been when we came home from school. I don't think we had opened the windows since she'd been gone. Sometimes after school you could still smell her when you got home.

"I don't have a choice," Dad snapped. "There's going to be some layoffs at work. The warehouse is downsizing." He sighed and paced. "They've cut my hours. I have to make sure we don't lose everything." He wiped his hand over his face and beard. "I'm sorry, but you wouldn't understand."

Luke wiped his nose. He threw his handful of stones into the water.

"Try me," he said.

Dad sank his hands into his pockets. He stared at the back of Luke's hanging head.

"I've sold the house."

"Without telling us?"

"Look," he said, "we can't—*I* can't afford to stay where we are anymore. I'm trying my best."

"Try harder." Luke sniffed. "Isn't that what you'd say to me?"

Dad walked off, barely looking over his shoulder.

"It's the way it is, Luke, like it or not."

He shouldn't say things like that; he never used

to say things like that. It's not fair.

"When?" Luke shouted. "When do we have to move to this stupid place?"

Dad stopped and turned.

"Friday."

I felt the sob catch in my chest.

Luke was mad as anything.

"Why didn't you tell us before?"

Dad kept walking and muttered, "It's better this way."

ॐ Fourteen ॐ

When we got back, Luke phoned Grandma and Grandpa Hamblin. He sat on the stairs and asked them to tell Dad to change his mind.

Then he was silent for a long time, listening, holding the phone loosely by his ear. He said "no" or "yes" or "but" to them now and again, but they kept talking. I could hear their voices but not what they were saying, like a radio far away.

"They want to speak to you," said Luke.

But I squeezed past him to go upstairs while he held the phone out and watched me go to my room. I blocked my ears so I couldn't hear what he told them, so I didn't feel bad about leaving him there by himself. But it didn't work.

Luke didn't speak to Dad for days. I didn't either, of course. Dad didn't say anything about our not talking. He gave us each two packing boxes from work, told us to fill them with everything we wanted to keep. Just two boxes, no more. I'll bet he was like that at work. Because he was a supervisor in the warehouse, he could say what size box you had to use, do this, do that.

I packed up my boxes in a special way: books together, clothes together, shoes together, special things together, putting things in compartments with extra strips of cardboard so it was all divided up. Above my bed was a picture Mom and me had drawn. I had drawn her and she had drawn me. I rolled it up and put it in a small compartment by itself. Sometimes silence is really uncomfortable. Like trying to fit all your things into cardboard boxes.

Friday, and Mia and Daisy came running up to me. Mia looked excited, but she folded her arms and said, "You don't have to keep being such a sulker. You could ask someone else to sing in the concert with you."

And Daisy said, "She could ask to be in one of the big groups of singers." Then she laughed. "Oh, but the auditions are closed now anyway."

Then Mia stopped laughing with her.

"I think if you just said sorry for cheating so I couldn't do the sponsored silence and for being such a loser, then we'd let you play with us again. Well?" said Mia, her lips like the top of a gym bag, her eyes fierce. "Are you going to?"

She tapped her foot.

"If you don't say sorry, we won't tell you what we've found."

Daisy elbowed Mia. "I thought we weren't going to tell her we found a dog."

Mia gritted her teeth. "No! We *weren't* going to tell her we found a dog over by the gates."

"But you just did!" said Daisy.

Mia blinked hard. "No, you did!"

Daisy said, "But she's got to say sorry before we show her or say anything else."

Mia couldn't help herself. "It's the biggest dog in the world, and it's so friendly. It ate my cheese sandwich right out of my hand! I'm going to ask my mom if we can keep it."

They looked over to the school gates. So did I.

"It's gone!" Mia screeched. "That's your fault, Daisy!"

"No, it's not! It's Cally's fault. If she'd just said sorry right away like you asked, then we wouldn't have had to leave it all by itself for so long."

Mia grabbed my sleeve.

"Typical! You're always messing things up for me."

I ran, leaving Mia holding my empty gray cardigan and shrieking, "When I see it again, I'm never, *ever* going to tell you, ever again!"

I went to the library to get away from them and to read about dogs. I found out about Homeless, Irish wolfhound, ancient wolf hunter, loyal friend and protector; about precious silver collars and how in the olden days people paid high prices to own one. There was a story with a brown-and-white drawing of a famous wolfhound called Cu who saved his owner's child from a wolf. I looked at the pictures. I stared at the fearless guardian. That's what Homeless looked like—like he would go to the ends of the earth to save you.

I wished I could see him again. I wished he were mine.

❧ Fifteen ❧

I didn't go straight home after school on Friday. I went to the park.

She was still wearing her red raincoat and green hat when I saw her on the other side of the duck pond. Homeless was with her. He came bounding around the edge of the pond, straight to me. I saw how happy it made Mom.

If only dogs could talk. He could tell everyone that he'd seen her. Then they'd believe me. But then it was nice that he didn't talk, nice that he didn't say, "Why haven't you done your math homework? Why haven't you checked your spelling? Where're your gym clothes?"

We sat at the edge of the pond. His eyes traced the snow-white bread crumbs Mom showered on the water; his ears jumped up when she smiled at us.

I imagined I said, *Crumbs to find your way home,* and she laughed and said, *Just like Hansel and Gretel.*

Mom, I said inside, *will you find me again when we move? Will you bring Homeless with you?*

I leaned on Homeless and closed my eyes. Imagined it was her sitting there next to me, a kiss on my forehead, a strong, warm, breathing body next to mine. Homeless smelled like a toy rabbit I had when I was little. I laid my head on him, forgot about the time.

Then Luke was there, crouched beside me, saying they'd been looking for me everywhere. He patted Homeless, said, "Hello, boy, where did you come from?"

Mom wasn't there anymore. Homeless stood up, towered over us; his tail swayed as he licked Luke's hand.

"Dad's waiting around the corner in the moving van," Luke said. "We'd better get going before he sees the dog. He'll freak out. Where did you find him, anyway?"

Luke put his arm around me, made me leave Homeless behind. He held out a packet of bubble gum.

"You can make huge bubbles with these, big as a basketball," he said. "But you can't chew properly if you're crying. Come on, just try."

Dad pulled up in a big van by the park gates. He opened the window and called out, "Get in! I can't stop on double yellows."

We got in the van.

"Where's your school cardigan?" asked Dad.

Luke shook his head and said, "Dad, I think there's something wrong with Cally."

❧ Sixteen ❧

I woke up in the morning in my old bed in a new room. I could smell pancakes. Mom used to make pancakes. They meant: it's raining and it's going to rain all day, so let's stay in and eat goodies and watch TV. Or: it's a special day, like your birthday.

I crept out into the hallway. Dad and Luke were in the kitchen area, talking about me. They weren't making pancakes.

Dad said, "She's just taking the sponsored quiet a bit too far. You know what she's like."

"Sponsored silence. That was over a week ago; we gave her the money. Remember?"

"What about yesterday at the park? Surely she said something then." He sighed. "Where did I put the milk?"

"Dad, I'm telling you, she didn't say a word. I don't think she's said anything since you showed us the apartment last Saturday."

"She's just playing one of her silly games."

"Well, this game's even longer than Monopoly."

You can let people talk about you for only so long. I went into the kitchen area. Dad said good morning, which he never says. He asked me how I was, asked me if my throat was sore. Then he handed me a jug.

"Pop downstairs and ask our new neighbors if they can spare us some milk."

Dad let me out the door but left it open. I heard shuffling behind the door, and I knew they were listening.

From our apartment you go down the stairs, around the corner a bit, and then there is a long passageway to the backyard. In the passageway is the door to Apartment 1. Sweet frying smells squeezed out from around their shiny red door.

There was a spongy handle and a drum for a

door knocker. A stick was hanging from a piece of string pinned to the top of the doorframe. I looked at it for ages. Not because I didn't work out straightaway what you had to do. I just didn't know what tune to play. On the TV shows that Dad watches, the police bang hard three times, or five times if it's very serious. So I didn't want to do that. Then there's a *bang-de-bang-bang* that you do when you know them. Four quick knocks sound like a salesman or someone complaining. One bang wouldn't sound right. It might sound like someone dropping something.

Then the door opened. A barefoot lady with fair hair tied in a ponytail was holding a plate covered in silver foil.

"Oh! Hello!" she said, bright and happy. "You must be from upstairs. I was just on my way up. We made you some pancakes." She lifted the foil. "Hope there's enough. How many of you are there?"

I held up three fingers.

"What's that you've got there?"

I showed her the jug.

"Ah, I see," she said, taking a step back into their apartment. "You can never find anything on the first morning in a new place. Never mind, I'm sure we've got plenty to spare."

She shifted a blue bag on the floor by the door with her foot and beckoned me in.

Their apartment wasn't like ours. The walls were yellow and orange and green. Bits of silver foil fluttered around plastic tubes and wires. There were statues, feathers, stones, and bark scattered like junk all around the windowsills. Shelves were stacked sky high with boxes and games and models. Things shimmered and glowed and made you want to touch them. It made you think magic went on there.

There were sponges taped to the corners of the table, a big wooden table where a boy was sitting. When I first saw him, I just saw the dark shadows around his eyes in his moon-colored face, his long black bangs bunched up by a pair of blue swimming goggles he'd pushed up onto his forehead. His thin fingers felt around the bits and pieces of something he was making.

His mom stamped on the wooden floor.

"Sam," she called. He rolled his head toward us. Then she patted his shoulder, took his hand, and touched different parts of his fingers, a bit like typing on a keyboard.

"Our new neighbor's here," she said, tapping away. "It's a girl about your age. She looks very nice." She smiled and tapped again, then said, "She'd like some milk."

She took the jug from me and put Sam's hands around it. She snapped the goggles off his head and rolled her- eyes. Sam went into the kitchen area, running his hand against the wall on the way. His body weaved as he touched the things around him with the backs of his hands, his elbows, his hips, making contact all the time. Carefully he poured the milk with his fingers around the rim of the jug. When the milk touched his fingers, he stopped pouring and brought the jug back to his mom.

His mom said, "I'm Mrs. Cooper, and this is Sam; he's eleven. He's blind and mostly deaf, but otherwise he's just like you and me." She smiled and took my hand. "He likes to meet people in his own way. What's your name?"

I ran up the stairs. Without the milk. Without the pancakes. Shut my bedroom door and went under the covers. I didn't want to say my name. Sam didn't seem like me at all, and I didn't like it when his hand reached toward my face.

Soon there was a knock at our front door, and Dad opened it.

I heard Mrs. Cooper talking, telling him who she was and that she had a boy called Sam, and saying, "Here's some milk. Is that enough? And we made you some pancakes. Hope you like them."

The door closed, and Luke was whispering, "You should've asked her if Cally said anything."

Dad sighed. "She must have; we got some milk, didn't we?"

Soon there was another knock: Mrs. Cooper.

I heard her say, "Sorry to bother you again; it's just that Sam asked me to give these to your little girl."

Dad came in my room and stood there for a while. I stuck my hand out from under the duvet, and Dad dropped some things into it. I felt them, two flat circles of plastic with grooves all round the edge. Little cogs from a machine.

❧ Seventeen ❧

I only went back downstairs because Luke was going on and on at me, trying to make me speak, jumping out and trying to scare me, putting a cold key down my back. He was really getting on my nerves. And besides, when you've got two plastic cogs in your pocket, it makes you think that the thing they belong to is not going to work without them.

I crept downstairs without my shoes on, without telling Dad, while he was headfirst emptying another cardboard box.

I looked at the yellow skin of the drum for ages and listened at the door. I hoped it would just open by itself. I waited and waited. Did my twelve times table a few times. Waited some more. I decided two bangs would do.

I heard a happy shriek coming from inside.

Mrs. Cooper opened the door wide. The blue bag was on the floor again, right in the doorway. Mrs. Cooper rolled her eyes and kicked it out of the way. Sam was feeling along some shelves. He pulled out a cardboard box from a big stack, knocking some other things onto the floor. He said something, but his voice was strange, and I couldn't understand him. He held the box up. It was upside down, but I could see very clearly what it was.

Mrs. Cooper closed the door behind me and whispered, "He can't see, and he doesn't hear much, but I promise you he won't bite."

Sam was already at the dining table. He reached out and dragged another chair so it was right next to him. He wasn't really taking any notice of me. So I leaned on the chair.

He tipped the contents onto a tray. There was a clock face with numbers pegged into it, and Sam clipped it into another ring with raised bumps around the edge. The instructions on the box said the bumps were a kind of writing that Sam could feel. Silently he clipped and turned and snapped pieces onto the back of the clock. I felt the two cogs in my hand, tried to see if I could tell where they went just by touching them.

When it's that quiet, you can hear little creaks and ticks coming from the house. A bump from upstairs and the muffled sound of Dad's voice. The hum from the fridge. Me breathing. Sam breathing, quicker than me. Sam leaned closer, like he was trying hard to hear what sounds I was making. He had a little plastic tube clipped around and going into his left ear.

Mrs. Cooper came in with two mugs of juice, putting one of the mugs and a napkin right into Sam's hand. Sam leaned toward the sound of her footsteps as she left, swigged from his mug, then wiped his mouth on his sleeve. Even his long, floppy bangs didn't cover his grin.

He held his palm out to me, the juice still glistening on his sleeve. I knew what he wanted without his even saying anything.

I put the two cogs he'd given me into his skinny hand.

He smiled like he was looking at something inside himself or remembering something that made him feel good. It made me smile too. But he wouldn't have known that.

Mrs. Cooper came back to see the finished clock. Some of the cogs were in the wrong place, so she turned it over a few times, took off a few pieces, and guided Sam's hands. Sometimes Sam patted her hands away so he could do it himself, and when she tapped her fingers on his palm, he pushed her hands under the table. He leaned against me, until his face was close to mine and I could smell the juice on his breath and see the tiny dark hairs over his top lip. I already knew then that Sam didn't see things like we do, that the reason he leaned so close was that that was how the world talked to him—through his skin. He held the clock to his left ear, so it was between us. We listened to the perfect steady tick coming from inside. I saw how all the little pieces made one perfect thing.

On the table Sam had lots of little colored boxes with cards filed in them. They had words at the bottom and bumps punched in the top.

"It's called braille," said Mrs. Cooper. "It's a sort of writing Sam can feel."

Pictures were stuck on the cards with tape, gone yellowy brown. He laid some cards on the table. There was a picture of a frying pan with yellow circles inside saying PANCAKES, and a picture of a clock saying CLOCK, and another with a big number 2.

"Sam's got his own way of seeing things. He likes people to make up their own minds what he's saying," said Mrs. Cooper.

I knew Sam was saying they had made the pancakes so they could meet us and then Sam and me could make the clock.

There was a loud rapping at the door, just like a policeman. Mrs. Cooper opened the door wide.

"Is my daughter here?" Dad said.

"Oh, hello. Yes, she's been helping Sam. Come in."

Dad stayed in the passageway and said, "Cally didn't tell me where she was going."

Mrs. Cooper said, "I'm sorry, I didn't check." She whispered to him, while she smiled and winked at me. "She seems so shy and quiet."

Dad didn't say anything, just stared at me with

narrow eyes. Then he watched Sam as he came toward him holding two cards up, one saying PAN-CAKES and the other card saying GIFT. Sam rolled his head, turned his ear toward Dad. I suppose he meant the pancakes were like a present. But I wasn't sure.

"Thanks for the pancakes," Dad said, biting his lip.

He flicked his head. "Cally, come on, there's some unpacking to do."

Mrs. Cooper said, "Well, if there's anything else I can do . . . Cally's welcome, anytime."

But Dad was already halfway up the stairs.

❧ Eighteen ❧

Later Dad said, "Let's take a walk. Luke? You coming?"

We walked across the common, along the open grass, following a path between wide ancient trees and skinny white tree trunks and tangled brambles and bracken. Magpies bounced and flew away in a clearing where we found a bench. The bench leaned backward and was sinking into the soft ground.

Dad nudged me. "What's that boy's name?"

"Sam," said Luke. Dad rolled his eyes at him. He wasn't supposed to answer.

"What's wrong with him, anyway?" asked Luke.

Dad sighed. He shook his head. "It's not that there's something *wrong* with him; he just can't see and hear. Is that right, Cally?"

I nodded.

Luke spun his Frisbee and ran after it. He threw it again toward a girl twirling around a low tree branch.

Dad folded his arms. We sat and watched an old man stoop and shuffle across the open space between the trees. Trees grew higher up out of a steep bank past the long grass. A long way off you could see the tops of banks and churches in town.

"Used to be a park with a lake over there," Dad said, pointing, "just beyond the trees. Swan Lake it was called. When I was a kid, I used to take my model boat there. I made it myself."

Dad laughed. "It sank. It's probably still down there, rotting away. They closed the park down ages ago. I can't remember why."

He didn't talk like this very often anymore. I liked it. I leaned against him.

"There was a miniature steam train that used to run around the park at the top of the bank." He leaned over to see me follow his finger pointing at the high trees. He laughed again. "Some of us kids didn't have a penny between us, so we'd jump on the back when the driver wasn't looking."

He looked at me, smiled.

"I used to make up stories about having my own train and who I'd take with me to the places I wanted to see: mountains and waterfalls and lakes, the glaciers in Iceland."

In my mind's eye I could see him leaning from a train window, the rattling, thumping beat of wheels against the tracks.

"All kids make up stories, about all sorts of things. I think it's just because they wish things were different."

He nudged me. "I wish things were different too."

And for a minute I thought if Dad wished things were different, that meant he'd talk about Mom and remember her and make it feel like she was here. And I was ready to say, "Okay, Dad, can we get the photos out and talk about Christmases and birthdays and vacations together and get your guitar and try to sing Mom's songs so it isn't like she's never been here at all?"

And then Dad said, "But we've got to forget the past and making up silly stories. It's all part of growing up."

He sounded like Mrs. Brooks, so I didn't listen. Maybe she'd told him what to say. Instead I watched Luke fling his Frisbee, closer and closer to the girl in the tree, who was hanging upside down by her knees.

Dad went on. "So first job is to paint your bedroom. What color do you want?"

Now the girl was going around and around the branch; her long brown hair flicked after her. Luke leaned on the tree.

"Pink, I suppose," Dad said. "Girls like pink, don't they?"

I kicked a pile of rabbit poop on a hump of grass by the bench. When you haven't been speaking for a little while, even though the color of your bedroom is normally really important, it just doesn't seem to matter. I shrugged. I know he just wanted me to say something. Not anything that was really important, though; not anything he didn't want to hear. Actually I didn't like pink anymore. You sort of grow out of it. I tried to imagine my bedroom any other color but pink and the boring old-book-page color it was.

I watched the girl sit up on the branch; Luke climbed up beside her. She pulled her headband down around her neck, straightened her hair, and put it on again.

"Are you still not speaking to me? After everything I just said?" Dad said.

Dad leaned back; we leaned with it as the bench sank further. Dad stood up and found a stone to put under the bench leg where the concrete had crumbled.

"Must be all the rain we've been having. Worn it away. I should talk to the council about that," he muttered, looking around as if somebody might be nearby and he could tell that person to fix the problem.

He sighed and looked at me.

"You know, sooner or later you're going to have to speak. How else are you going to get what you want?"

❧Nineteen❧

Dad and Luke were rearranging furniture. We had a two-seater sofa and two armchairs. You couldn't see the TV very well whichever way around they moved them. Or you couldn't get from the kitchen area to the sitting room part without climbing over the back of the sofa.

Dad muttered, "There's not enough room to swing a cat."

Luke said, "We haven't got a cat."

"It's a figure of speech, Luke."

"I'm not stupid; I know what it means."

"We've got too much stuff, so cat or no cat,

something's got to go. We'll have to do without one of the armchairs."

"But that means there'll only be three seats."

"Well, there's only three of us, Luke. Three seats, three people; do the math."

"But what if someone comes to visit?"

"Like who?"

Luke huffed and rolled his eyes. He said under his breath, "No wonder Cally doesn't want to speak to you."

"Well, I don't know, do I?" Dad muttered.

Dad and Luke carried the armchair downstairs. They left it outside the front with a note saying Free to Good Home.

Dad packed up Mom's old cooking equipment because we didn't have enough cupboards for them to live in. He packed up the books and photo albums and his guitar, mumbling that it was broken; all the things that hadn't been touched for over a year were put back into the boxes.

Dad looked at his watch and said he had to go meet up with some people from work.

"Find somewhere for those boxes, Luke. I won't be long."

But Luke didn't. He was too busy on his computer, swerving racing cars around corners. So I took them, to make sure we kept everything; dragged the armchair through the passageway, and tipped it sideways to get it through the back door; and put everything in the shed. I took my drawing things and put them in there too.

All the walls were browny orange in the shed, and it smelled of new paint. It had been empty except for a big umbrella. I tucked my feet under, curled up in the armchair. It was like having my own house, big inside and full of important things.

I drew a picture of Homeless with Mom in her raincoat and hat and left an empty bubble for her to say something. I looked at the picture and imagined telling Mom what color I wanted my bedroom painted, and she said, *Just like the depths of the ocean, or the evening sky.* I said, *How come you can't see stars in the daytime?* And she said, *I was never any good at science, but I do know that lights shine best in the dark.* And I said, *That's why we have fireworks at night,* and she laughed.

❧ Twenty ❧

"We need to do something about your breathing," boomed Mr. Crisp at the end of Monday's music lesson. "Especially those of you singing in the end-of-term concert."

He was in charge of singing, plays, and concerts and, I thought, general happiness. He had misty white hair and a belly full of laughter.

"Think of it like this: we're full of air."

"No, we're not, sir. We're mostly water!"

"Daniel Bird, this isn't a science lesson; it's music. Different rules apply."

"But that's what Miss Steadman said."

Mr. Crisp could make one eyebrow go up.

"If you want to be totally scientific about it, we're mostly made of space, and a space is where the sounds need to come out. Now, everyone, open your mouth wide. You should be able to fit two fingers in the gap. That's two fingers, Daniel Bird, not your whole hand!"

He slapped his round belly.

"Good! Now put your hands on either side of your belly button, fill your lungs, feel your belly expand. Daniel, you can take your fingers out now."

I opened my mouth when we were supposed to sing. But no sounds came out. I didn't let them.

"Hmm, better, those of you who tried," said Mr. Crisp, doing that thing with one eyebrow again. "You know, sounds end up coming out of your mouth, but they start with the air much, much farther down."

Then the bell rang, and he said, "Cally Fisher, I'd like to speak to you a minute."

He sat and beckoned me over.

"I've noticed your name's not down for the concert," he said when everyone had gone. "Conspicuous by your absence, as they say. I would've thought you'd like to stand up in front of everyone and sing your heart out."

He tapped his fingers over his mouth and then along an electronic keyboard, like it was helping him think. No sound came out; it wasn't plugged in.

"Remember when we did *Charlotte's Web* in third grade? Your performance, your magnum opus. Remember?"

Even I remembered my lines from two years ago. Charlotte, the spider (that was me in a padded black costume with long legs held up on sticks), had made her egg sac, filled with five hundred eggs. Harry Turner was Wilbur, the pig, and he had to say, "What's a magnum opus?" and I had to say, "It means a great work; it's the finest thing I ever did."

"Remember?" Mr. Crisp said, looking up as if he could see the past in the ceiling. "You made your mom proud that day. And I know she would have loved to see you in *Olivia!* last year."

He stopped for a moment, so we both could think about why she hadn't been able to be there, so the sadness didn't have to come out. When he started talking again, his voice was rich and warm, from deep in his belly.

"You know she came in to see me a few days before the show. She didn't tell me what it was, but she said she had a surprise planned for you, to show how much your singing meant to her."

I never found out what it was either. But what he said made my heart feel wide. I knew he was thinking of exactly the time he saw her, because it made the words full of her, breathed her alive, brought her to me, to us.

"So, Miss Fisher, it's not too late, if you still want to sing. I'm prepared to make an exception in this case."

He waited a minute.

He ran his fingers the whole way along the keyboard and then slapped his hands in his lap.

"Off you go then, but remember, you can come back and see me anytime."

He plugged in the cord and started playing.

His hair billowed like a thick mist. I walked slowly to the door. I liked that he didn't go on at me or look disappointed. I liked the music he made.

As I opened the door, he stopped playing. He held out his arms to show the drums and tambourines, the recorders and guitars, the rows of silent keyboards, and called out, "You know, unless some-one uses these instruments, they're just shapes of wood and plastic and metal. I think you can still make your mom proud."

❧ Twenty-One ❧

Sam was leaning on the gate when I came home from school. He reached out and swept his hand over my face so he knew who I was. I pushed the gate, and he laughed as he swung away.

He had an old-fashioned camera with him. He held the camera up to his face, one hand on my shoulder, and pressed the button. While I watched, the camera whirred and out rolled a grayish, shiny piece of paper. Then a photograph magically appeared. My chin was missing, but it was a nice picture of most of my face and the huge green common behind me. Then we swapped places, so I could take a picture of him.

We went inside, and Sam gave Mrs. Cooper the photographs. She had a machine like a typewriter but with only six keys and a big one in the middle. It punched the braille bumps into the cards, and she stuck my picture on one.

"You really don't say much, do you?" she said. "How about you write your name on it instead?"

Writing isn't like talking, and it's good for telling someone something without saying it. On the card instead of writing my name, I wrote: *Sam is my friend.*

Mrs. Cooper tapped the message on Sam's hand.

Sam gave a marker to Mrs. Cooper (because he doesn't find writing easy) and tapped out what he wanted her to write for him on his picture. Mrs. Cooper gave me the card and went off to make tea.

She had written for Sam: "*Cally and Me, one who feels and one who sees.*" It was like a little poem. I thought I knew which one was me and which one was him.

I looked closer at the picture I wanted to keep.

There was Sam, my new friend, grinning from under his floppy dark hair, the huge green common and trees behind him, and another familiar shape in the background. A silver-gray dog.

My insides lurched; my head felt like it would pop; I could feel my breath caught tightly at the top of my chest. Sam leaned close, tipped his left ear; he put his hand on my arm. He looked thoughtful; he seemed to know something was up. He pulled his boxes of cards over, opened the lids, found a card with the word WHAT?

Sam smoothed his fingers across the bumps on each card I handed him. DOG—Sam nodded. BIG—Sam nodded. I couldn't find a card for *homeless*, so I gave him the card for LOST.

Sam's eyebrows bunched up. So I pulled him outside, made him stand where he had been standing, held his arm out, rolled his fingers under until just his first finger was pointing across the common. Homeless was still there, far away, his nose to the ground. I climbed on the wall, made myself as big as possible in a star shape, waved and laughed and laughed. Homeless's head rose; his ears twitched forward. And then he came, slowly at first, then galloping straight to us across the common.

I put Sam's hand on Homeless, but he never let go of me. I felt his hand tighten around mine as he felt all over the tall body, felt for the right way to smooth Homeless's scruffy fur. Homeless let him touch his great teeth and cool, damp nose, find the end of his curved tail. Sam was jittery and laughing. I don't suppose he'd ever felt anything quite like Homeless before, and I was glad they'd met, that I had someone to share Homeless with. I smoothed Homeless's ears. Soft as my mom's hair.

Sam took two photographs of Homeless because the first one had just his tail and back legs. Homeless just wouldn't keep still, winding around us as if he had to keep us together.

"Wait!" Sam suddenly said.

He left me with Homeless, went inside, bumping into the doorway in his hurry to go in. He came out with some cheese and slices of ham, and Homeless wolfed them down.

Sam put his hand where his heart would be, patted his chest, then put one of his cards in my hand.

Sam stopped moving. He was so still, I wondered if he'd fallen asleep standing up.

I looked at the card. It had a picture just like the one on the Apartment to Rent sheet Dad had showed us. A picture of 4 Albert Terrace. It said HOME.

❧ Twenty-Two ❧

Then Mrs. Cooper came out. She said, "It's nearly dinnertime." Her eyes popped wide when she saw Homeless.

"Goodness!" she said. "Where did he come from?"

Sam went quiet. His face was serious. He held his hand out for Mrs. Cooper to tap what she was saying.

"You don't often see Irish wolfhounds these days." She laughed. "Not much call for them, what with there being no wolves here anymore. I think he must be lost, don't you?"

She checked for a collar, but he didn't have one.

"We ought to find out who he belongs to, although I can't imagine how anyone could lose something quite so big."

Homeless sat down. He looked into my face. He seemed to know something wasn't right.

"Somebody will be missing him. I'd better make some phone calls."

Sam didn't let go of Homeless; he didn't let go of me while Mrs. Cooper went in to make the calls.

And then Dad arrived.

"How did that dog get here?" he snapped.

"The children found him," said Mrs. Cooper, coming back out.

"But what's it doing here?"

Mrs. Cooper blinked. "I thought we'd better check if he was lost."

"And?"

"And I checked, and nobody's reported him missing."

Dad took a deep breath, fixed his eyes on me. "You going to tell me what's going on?"

I put my arms around Homeless, looked into his soft brown eyes, looked into Dad's icy blue ones. Sam still didn't let go of me, but he held my hand up with the card saying HOME, turned his left ear toward Dad.

Dad closed his eyes.

"No," he said, "we're not keeping it."

And I wished and hoped and tried to believe. Would anything that I said make him say yes?

I put my hands together like a prayer.

"No! We can't afford it."

Sam spelled something on his mom's hand.

"What about if we shared the cost?" said Mrs. Cooper.

"I said no!" Dad growled, and glared. "And right now I've got enough problems."

Mrs. Cooper said quietly, "Such a shame this all seems a problem," making Dad's mouth screw tight.

It wasn't like him to bite his tongue, but you could tell what he was thinking. It was written all over his face. *Stop interfering, mind your own business and get out of my winter cave!*

He looked at me once more.

"No!" he shouted.

Homeless's ears pricked at a whistling sound. He looked over his shoulder. Someone was standing by the trees, a small dark figure in a purple, puffy jacket, but I was the only one who saw him: Jed. Homeless slipped through my hands, through the open gate, and ran.

Mrs. Cooper sighed. "Oh, well, problem solved. For now."

Dad glared at her and said, "Someone else can sort it out. They'll soon forget all about it."

Forget is one of the words I hate. I know what it means: it's when you can't remember. And when you can't remember, you're not as good as when you can.

Dad pushed between us, called back without looking, "Cally, come inside now."

Mrs. Cooper whispered to me, "I'm sorry. I think I made things worse."

Sam tapped on Mrs. Cooper's hand. I could see she was making sense of the taps and shapes on her hand, listening to something.

She shrugged, smiled. "Sam says don't worry. You're not alone."

✨ Twenty-Three ✨

Dad was lying on the sofa watching TV, his shirt untucked, a bottle of beer in his hand.

"We can't have a dog here," he said.

He sat up, put the bottle down, and pressed the Mute button.

"We can't afford it. You'd want it to have a good home, wouldn't you?"

There was no point in trying to persuade him. No point in speaking to him at all. I folded my arms and watched a woman crying and shouting silently on the screen. A policeman was shouting back. Both of them were trapped behind the glass.

"I suppose this is going to be another reason for you to continue not speaking, is it?"

For the first time I could hear a crack in Dad's voice.

The woman on TV was running from a big explosion, and the policeman was shooting into the flames. Dad stood in front of the TV and switched it off. The fire faded into blackness.

"Look, if you just tell me what's going on, then maybe I can do something about it."

Dad rolled his eyes, realized what he'd said.

"Okay. I can't do anything about moving here or that dog. I've told you why." He crouched down in front of me. "Cally, please, just say something."

I tried to will him to know how much more it was. You can't just forget about things that mean so much to you. Even though Mom had died, he made it seem like we never knew her at all, like she never even existed. But she was here. I saw her, I felt her, especially when I was with Homeless.

"Has something happened at school?"

He waited.

"Please, say something."

I looked into his eyes. I could see a tiny dark

silhouette of me. Inside I said, *Mom, I love that dog,* and she said, *I know.*

Then Dad went to the fridge, got another bottle of beer, said, "You know, this not talking isn't very clever. It's not clever at all."

I remembered when we all went to the river near the big yellow cathedral. There was a boathouse with an open window. Swans were waiting there. Two of them reached their necks up and pulled a blue rope to ring a bell hanging from the window frame. They were mute swans. They didn't speak or squawk. They used the bell to tell someone they were hungry.

Mom said, "What beautiful creatures. Can you see how clever they are to find a way to speak to us like that, to speak of everything about themselves?"

And I felt the churning and the yearning inside for how Dad had been back then. How he'd listened to her and looked at her. How he had seen all of us, seen the way we wondered at the swans, and had said, "I see it too."

❧Twenty-Four❧

Jessica Stubbs brought in a folded note at afternoon attendance and I could tell by the way Miss Steadman looked up that the note was about me. She came over when it was quiet in math and we were doing some difficult division.

"Mrs. Brooks wants to see you before you go home. I think you know what it's about."

Mrs. Brooks had a new pair of sunglasses perched on her head. She came down the corridor carrying a trash can liner tied into a bundle. The air trapped inside made it into a puffy black balloon. She was walking with a lady from the office, saying, "If you could find the caretaker, let him know I need to see him. Straightaway!"

Mrs. Brooks came into her office, opened the window, and left the bag there.

She huffed loudly, sat down hard in her chair, said, "First, we need to talk about the fact that Miss Steadman tells me you're not participating in lessons."

Her new sunglasses had black lenses with white around the outside.

"Can you tell me what this is all about?"

There was a long silence.

"You know, all this not talking is starting to become a bit of a problem."

She waited.

"What about that dog on the playing field? Does that have something to do with you?"

She linked her fingers and leaned across her desk.

"I mean to get to the bottom of this, because that dog's been into school again and left a nasty mess. Daisy Bouvier's new shoes are ruined."

She nodded toward the trash can liner. She polished her sunglasses, sighed and waited, then said, "I think it's about time we asked your dad to come in for a chat."

❧ Twenty-Five ❧

"You can go exploring on the common on one condition," said Mrs. Cooper. She gave me an alarm clock. "When that rings, you're to come home."

I nodded. Me and Sam had a plan. I'd given Sam cards saying BIG, DOG, and FIND, and he'd nodded like mad. He went to ask his mom if we could go by ourselves.

Mrs. Cooper tapped on Sam's hand, pulled the blue bag off his back. There were other conditions.

"And you're not to let him go swimming, Cally," she said.

I nodded. Sam didn't want to know. He pulled his

hand away from his mom and went over to the wall, felt for the calendar hanging there. The dates were in normal writing with braille bumps on each box. I watched Sam's fingers run over the boxes and stop where a red sticker circle had been stuck.

"It's dangerous for Sam to swim in chlorine or cold water because it makes his asthma bad," said Mrs. Cooper with her hands on her hips. She looked hard at Sam, went over, and took his hand away from scratching at the sticker and trying to peel it off.

"Really bad," she said again. "A wade in the stream is fine, but nothing more."

She smoothed Sam's hair and sighed.

"Let Cally push you in the buggy."

Sam huffed and shook his head, but she soon persuaded him he was going in the buggy or not at all. Sam's buggy was a bit like a baby's stroller with three wheels. It was black and faded with orange raggedy pockets that Mrs. Cooper had filled with bottles of juice, shopping bags with some snacks, Sam's inhaler, and the alarm clock. When Sam sat in it, his knees were up high and his elbows stuck out the sides. I could see why he didn't want to go in it.

Mrs. Cooper chewed her thumb while she watched us cross the quiet road and bump onto the open common with all the just-in-case things and Sam's boxes of cards on his lap.

Sam stuck his arms out, and I pushed left or right, straight ahead, or around in circles—wherever he pointed. He reached for the bracken, the long grass, the tree trunks we passed. Softly he hummed, changing pitch when we went over bumps, down-hill, or uphill. Sometimes he just laughed and laughed or waved me to go faster.

Suddenly he sat up straight and pointed both his arms down for me to stop. He held up a card: WATER. We were by the stream and little brick bridge where Luke had gone when we first saw the apartment.

Sam took off his socks and shoes and waded in. He walked against the flow, bent over so his fingers trailed in the water. He looked like he belonged there.

I met him coming out the other side, and he pushed me gently to sit in the stroller, went around the back, and leaned on the handle with his skinny middle. He rested his hands on my shoulders so he could feel me lifting my arms to point left or right. At first I didn't know where to go. But I decided on the far side of the common, where I'd seen Homeless run, and soon we were pushing between the trees and bushes in the green gloom and standing in front of a gate.

Swan Lake was spelled out in curled metal writing along the top of tall rusted gates. Heavy links of chain with a chunky padlock were wound around them to keep them closed.

We left the stroller in a bush, took all our belongings in the shopping bags, and I helped Sam, step by step. We crawled in through a hole, over the crumbled bricks and creeping ivy, under the tangle of branches. We pushed through the bushes, came out in an opening.

There was a small building. Green paint peeled off the door like sunburned skin so you could see it used to be painted red underneath. Brick steps led up from beside the boarded window to the trees at the top of the bank. They circled high above a black, silent lake in the middle.

Sam reached out and felt along the wall. I led

him inside the open door. It must have been the ticket office for the old miniature railway Dad had told me about. There was a wide counter under the window. A broom with a broken handle leaned against the wall by a camping stove, some plates, a saucepan, and a big chipped dog bowl. Shopping bags and strips of cardboard were folded and piled neatly with a marker pen on top. The top one said HOMELESS. In the corner thick bundles of newspapers were laid out in a long rectangle, some blankets on top, made up into a bed. Next to it was the skin from a snake, shriveled dry. You could see each transparent scale, outlined in white, the dark holes where its eyes once searched for sunlight. I put it in Sam's hands. He smoothed its still head.

I found cards for Sam—BIG, DOG—and, because I couldn't find the right words, gave him GONE. Then: MAN and FRIEND, because I guessed Jed lived here with Homeless. But I couldn't stop wondering why Mom had brought Homeless to school, wondering why I had seen her walking with Jed in town.

Sam wanted to go to the lake. It was like he knew it was there even though it didn't make a sound, even though he couldn't touch it. I led him down to the edge. He called, the way you do when you go through a tunnel. His voice bounced around the banks, came back to us gently.

Mom was there, standing on the far side, her red coat vivid. I imagined in my silent heart she could hear me across the still water. *Is Homeless with you?* I asked her. *Have you seen him?* And she smiled and said, *Yes, I have. And one day he'll find you.*

Sam closed his eyes. I think he was listening in his heart too. The tops of the trees shushed as if we should stay quiet in this forgotten place.

I wanted to tell Sam about Jed, how I saw him with my mom and that Homeless had been with both of them. But his cards didn't have the right words or any of the little words that we use in between. And anyway, just then Mrs. Cooper's loud alarm clock went off. Even Sam jumped. We both knew we had to go back, that there wasn't time to go farther.

Mrs. Cooper hugged Sam like he'd been gone for a hundred years. It made me think he'd never been out without her before. He wriggled and wiped her kisses away. Somehow he looked different, and I felt different too. Like we'd started a journey, an adventure or something, and because we'd been together, because of that, it made us stronger.

❧ *Twenty-Six* ❧

Next evening Dad was going out with some friends from work and asked Mrs. Cooper if she'd keep an eye out for me. Luke was instructed to tell me to go to bed after he had watched a DVD.

Sam and me sat outside on the front wall with our faces turned to the sky. I knew Sam couldn't see what I could see, but I wondered if he could tell how far away things are. Maybe in his darkness he knew all about infinity. The sky was just dark enough to show the twinkling eye of the brightest star. *Are you up there?* I whispered in my mind. *Can you see me?*

Long black shadows stretched across the grass toward us. I nudged Sam, breathed in deep because my heart was thumping so hard. Homeless came padding out of the shadows. Two figures walked behind him: Mom and Jed.

They all stopped a little way away. I couldn't tell if Jed could see her, if he knew she was there. Mom reached into her pocket. I thought I saw her lips moving, I thought she might be saying something to Jed, but he didn't look at her. And then she was gone, just as if someone had blown out the birthday candles.

Jed and Homeless came close.

Sam slid off the wall, and Jed let him feel around his face. Jed's eyes were bright as Sam turned his palms up and bounced his hands up and down as if he were throwing something. Jed laughed, a soft laugh.

"Hello," said Mrs. Cooper, coming out with two mugs of hot chocolate. "I know you. Seen you in town often enough. You tried to teach Sam and me to juggle a couple of times."

The corners of Jed's eyes crinkled so you knew he was smiling.

"Hello," he said softly.

Mrs. Cooper put the mugs down and tapped on Sam's hands. He nodded madly. He already knew who Jed was.

Mrs. Cooper looked at Homeless, lying on his back with his belly in the air, his pink tongue curled, his ears fallen back.

"Is he your dog?" she said to Jed. "He came here the other day. We thought he was a stray."

"I look after him," Jed said, and he kept smiling. "Sometimes I have to leave him on his own for a bit."

"Is there anything we can do for you, food or blankets? I can call the animal shelter or someone if you're having difficulties looking after the dog."

Jed ruffled Homeless and shook his head.

"Just hungry," he said.

Mrs. Cooper went in and came out with some fruitcake and a mug of tea for Jed. She gave Homeless some corned beef straight from the can, then asked Jed if he had everything he needed.

He looked at me; his eyes were warm and

friendly. He nodded and whispered, "I think so."

We all sat on a blanket and leaned against the wall and watched the night sky stealing the light. Mrs. Cooper chatted away to Jed about how much it had been raining considering it was nearly the start of summer. Then we were quiet as we blew on our hot drinks. I saw the steam rising, disappearing.

Then Sam suddenly said something, the clearest I ever heard him speak.

"Whose dog is he?"

"He's Jed's dog, Sam," said Mrs. Cooper, tapping.

Sam shook his head. Jed was shaking his head too.

"Whose dog?" said Sam louder, pulling at Jed's arm.

The stars seemed to have fallen from the sky and were in Jed's eyes, and I just knew he was going to say something beautiful. I saw Mrs. Cooper spell what Jed said to me on Sam's hand.

"I'm his guardian, if you like," he said, looking into my eyes. "But he belongs with you."

❧ Twenty-Seven ❧

D ad was waiting for me after school the next day. I had to stand outside the classroom while he talked to Miss Steadman and Mrs. Brooks. Miss Steadman kept looking through the doorway and in the end came out to give me a crossword puzzle. She smiled and closed the door behind her. I couldn't do the puzzle.

Dad was in there for ages. And even then we didn't go home. We had another appointment.

The doctor pressed my tongue down with a tongue depressor, prodded around my neck, took my temperature. He said he couldn't find anything wrong with me and that Dad was doing the right thing by talking to the people at school. He was going to send a report to the school, and the school would contact an expert called Dr. Colborn, a psycho or something like that.

Dad looked more worried when we left than when we went in. And it made me feel scared of Dr. Colborn. I started to think that she was going to make me tell her that I saw my dead mom and then tell me it wasn't true and make me say it wasn't true. And worse, if I said it wasn't true, it might make Mom go away forever, and then I might never see Homeless again. Already I hated Dr. Colborn.

We still didn't go home. Dad said he needed to go back in to work to catch up on what had happened at a meeting. The bus dropped us outside the warehouse.

Five men were waiting outside, the top halves of their blue overalls tied by the arms around their waists. They hardly lifted their heads as Dad passed.

"How did it go?" Dad said.

"You're too late," one of them said. "We're out. All of us."

Dad told me to wait outside under the awning. He went in, slammed the door behind him, and started shouting. Rain drummed on the metal roof. It sounded like a war had started. I covered my ears, but there was pounding and hammering coming from inside too.

Luke was waiting to speak to Dad when we got home. His voice was shaky; his eyes were wide and glassy.

"A couple of guys from your work came by. They said they wanted to speak to you. Has something bad happened?"

Dad hid behind his hands, rubbed around his face, and took his time before he spoke.

"They've all lost their jobs."

Luke's voice cracked. "Does that mean you too? Are we going to have to move again?"

"It's not that—"

Dad moved quickly, hooked his elbow around Luke's neck, pulled him in.

"It's okay—I've still got my job. It's just I promised I'd look after them."

❧ Twenty-Eight ❧

Dad was hanging over a cup of coffee in the kitchen, sealing a white envelope. He said he needed to go and talk to a few people. His voice was frosty; he looked more crumpled than ever.

"There's some money on the table. Luke, get anything you need from the shop. Mrs. Cooper said you could both spend the day with them."

"My friend Rachel is coming over," said Luke.

Dad muttered he was sure Mrs. Cooper wouldn't mind and something about her taking in any waifs and strays.

Luke waited by the front door for Rachel. I

banged twice on the drum, and Mrs. Cooper called out to come on in. Sam's blue bag was on the floor by the door as usual. I looked inside it. It was Sam's swimming stuff: swimming shorts, a towel, and goggles. It made me think Sam was the kind of person who'd never give up.

We knew when Rachel had arrived because of the sound coming from the door. Me and Sam leaned against the back of the door and felt the drumming through the wood, the rhythm thumping something bright and strong, like a dance against our skin. It was as if someone important had arrived, like when the music starts before the show begins.

I opened the door. It was the girl I'd seen twirling around the tree on the common.

"That's my sister," said Luke. "Cally doesn't speak. She can, but she doesn't. And that's Sam. I don't think he speaks either." He looked embarrassed. Like we should be avoided.

"I like your drum," Rachel said.

Luke shook his head, muttered, "I don't think he can hear you."

She breezed in. "Anyone want to do face paints?"

I could see straightaway why Luke liked her, but why she wanted to hang around with him I didn't know.

Mrs. Cooper laid out packets of food and recipes on the table while we sat on the floor and painted our faces (except Luke, of course). Sam painted his blue, and he looked like an alien; my face was the yellow sun with the rays going down my neck and out to my ears; Rachel drew flowers on her forehead. She blew on her fingers, painted like grass, and danced them around in front of her face. She looked as if she were made of music, the way she swayed.

Mrs. Cooper said, "Seeing as it's raining, how would you all like to do some cooking?"

Luke rolled his eyes, but Rachel smiled at him over her shoulder, made him want to.

I fetched one of the boxes from the shed. There was a food mixer, a whizzy thing, and a chopping machine. There was a set of red plastic mixing bowls and spoons that Dad had given Mom for her birthday. They fitted inside one another like Russian dolls. I thought we could just borrow them.

Me and Sam made cakes (but he was mostly

interested in licking the bowl under the table), and Luke and Rachel made two pizzas, while Mrs. Cooper put her feet up on the sofa and read a book. Rachel pretended we were in a restaurant, calling out orders for extra chocolate and more cheese.

Mrs. Cooper hummed away to the radio while she washed the equipment and wiped up the mess.

I wrote a note for her and put it on the box: *For Mrs. Cooper.*

"It was a very good idea of yours, saved a lot of stirring and chopping," she said, drying a mixing bowl. "But I think we should check with your dad first."

Well, what would be the point of that?

She put the clean machines back in the box, with one eye on me. Before she closed the lid, she leaned against the kitchen counter while she wrote a note with me watching: Did these belong to your mom? I nodded. Dad must have told her. She left the point of the pen on the dot under the question mark. She was thinking hard; you could see it in her eyebrows. She might have been thinking that I would want to talk about Mom. Then she wrote: Do you miss her? She didn't look very sure she should have written that either. But it was all right.

I shook my head. I didn't miss her like I used to. Not now that I'd seen her. But it suddenly made me think that was all I did: see her. It's not the same as being with someone. You might just as well have a photograph. It made me think of Homeless. What was so nice about him was that he went with you, and he moved; he smelled like your oldest teddy bear that nobody is allowed to wash. The wiry fur on his back was warm scrunched in your hand.

Mrs. Cooper gave me a squeeze and said, "I can't quite imagine your dad's into making cookies and cupcakes!"

She smiled and wrote again: If he says yes, then I would like them very much.

"Food's ready!" she called.

We had a picnic on the floor. Afterward Rachel and Luke went to beat Sting on his computer racing game, and Mrs. Cooper went outside to hang out the laundry.

Sam drummed on the floorboards with his hands, tried to find the rhythm Rachel had made. His breath rattled and whistled in his throat. And then everything went quiet. He lay down. I saw the blue paint on his face; I saw his blue lips.

"Find Mom," he whispered.

I ran out to Mrs. Cooper. The sheets wrapped around her like ghostly clouds.

"Hello, sunshine," she said, quickly looking at my yellow painted face while she grappled with the flapping clothes.

The breeze dropped the sheets. Mrs. Cooper saw me frozen. She ran into the apartment before I could tug at her sleeve.

❧ Twenty-Nine ❧

Mrs. Cooper gave Sam his inhaler, rocked him on her lap.

"I'm supposed to look for the pink color returning to your cheeks," she said, trying to laugh.

"Oh, Sam," she whispered. "What's going on? This seems to be happening more often."

She saw he was getting better, puffed up some pillows, and patted the window seat, saying, "Just do something together quietly."

Sam was by his calendar, whispering to himself. He found today's date and ran his fingers across the squares one by one. I thought he might be reading or maybe counting days. He stopped at the square with the sticker.

I picked up Sam's skinny white hand. He had blue stringy veins on his wrist and chocolate under his fingernails. I pointed to each finger, trying to remember what I'd seen Mrs. Cooper do. Sam smiled.

We were there for hours. Mrs. Cooper gave me a laminated sheet that had pictures of hands showing what you had to do. She said she thought it was a great idea for us two to have a chat.

It took ages to learn the deaf-blind alphabet, and I had to keep looking at the pictures to check what to do, but it was really easy. My name was: scoop from thumb to first finger, touch the thumb, touch the middle of the palm twice for two *L*'s, and touch the pad below the thumb. Sam's name was easy to remember because it had only three letters: hook the little finger (a bit like a pinkie swear, except with your pointing finger), touch your thumb, and then put three fingers on your palm. Sam showed me on my hand. At first I had to write down the letters he was making one at a time so I could keep up. Sam was very patient. It's hard to say what's happening when someone's touching your hand and making letters. It's sort of feeling-listening.

Then Sam spelled out a question. Just like that, he came out and asked me.

"Why don't you speak?"

I'd only ever heard his voice awkward and trapped in his throat. And he had never heard mine. It was like meeting him all over again but also, somehow, like he was my oldest friend, who I had known forever.

I didn't know what to tell him. So slowly I tapped on his hand, "I don't want to." But Sam doesn't give up.

"I don't want to be deaf and blind," he spelled.

"But you can hear some things."

He smiled.

"Once I heard a mouse."

I didn't know if he meant that he'd really heard it with his ears. I could see him remembering. He opened his palm as if it were sitting there, quivering. It wasn't there in his hand, but it was there, in his mind and heart. He lowered his hand to the floor, let it go, let it run and hide.

"What did it sound like?" I spelled.

"Like a tiny bit of fear."

I imagined it trembling, its heart beating faster and faster. I tried to imagine how Sam heard it. But his hearing was mysterious, buried somewhere deep inside him.

"Its heart beats five hundred times a minute," he spelled.

I sensed the quivering terror of its fragile life.

"Listen," he said.

He leaned his ear against the wall. I pressed my ear. I heard the crackle of my hair and then the silence of the still wall. I felt the tiny thumping of the mouse's anxious heart.

Sam tapped, "Can you feel how brave it is too?"

But he didn't seem to be talking about the mouse anymore.

✎ Thirty ✎

Sam had to rest for a couple of days, but it gave me time to practice the deaf-blind alphabet. It had been raining in bucket-loads, but now the sky was clear, the grass still glittering with the fallen rain.

I spelled on Mrs. Cooper's hand, "Can we go to the common?"

"Clever girl," she said. "You learn fast. Go on then, just for a little while."

She made us take the inhaler and the alarm clock and raincoats. We took snacks and drinks, and I took the alphabet sheet so I could feel-talk to Sam.

I pushed Sam out the front door across the open

grass, up and down the slopes, and between the overhanging bushes. We crawled through the crumbled wall at Swan Lake.

"What's there?" Sam spelled on my hand.

Slowly I spelled what I could see. I told him all the things Dad had said as if the park were still alive and people were strolling around the lake and a little boy were pulling a boat on a long piece of string and jumping on the back of the train as it whistled through the trees.

"What else?" Sam spelled.

I put my thumb and finger at either end of Sam's pointing finger, touched his fourth finger, put the side of my fist on his palm. It spells "dog." I heard the soft crackles of pine needles as Homeless limped between the trees by the black, silent lake. His head was hanging down, his fur mucky, dried blood around a big scratch across his nose. Then I saw the harsh graffiti words sprayed on the ticket office door, the splinters in the wood where some-one had tried to scratch them off. I saw the charred black sheets and ash left from Jed's burned news-paper bed. I was worried Jed might be hurt too and that Homeless had been left all alone.

I smoothed Homeless down, rubbed him gently; I washed his face with water from the lake and kissed his sad face. I let Sam know Homeless was hurt, spelled, "I promised your mom," and made him wait at the edge while I waded into the lake with Homeless, and he swam for a while as if the water were healing him. We held Homeless in our arms by the side of the lake with his damp head across our laps and covered him in a blanket of ferns.

I stroked Homeless, felt his warmth through the wet fur. His tail swished gently against the bracken. I kept Sam's hand in mine and spelled everything I could see. Almost everything.

She was sitting farther along, high up on the clay bank, bright and real. Mom turned and looked at me. *Mom,* I said in my mind, *Homeless needs to come and live with us.*

Her eyes glittered.

I don't know why I didn't go over. I don't know why I didn't reach out to touch her. Instead I wrapped my arms around Homeless, felt how strong he was. In my full heart I said, *You know what, Mom? This dog reminds me of you.*

Her warm, breathy laugh caught in the breeze, scattered in the clearing above the lake. A heron took off from its craggy perch on the broken trees at the center of the lake; its wide wings soared above the trees, and it was gone.

Sam spelled gently on my hand, "You have to find a way to keep him, look after him."

Mom smiled brightly at Sam. If he could have seen, he would have known she was looking straight at him and he was looking straight at her.

But we had to leave. We gave Homeless our snacks, and then he lay down by the ticket office and rested his head on his paws. He watched us go without wagging his tail. I wanted to promise him I'd find a way, but I didn't know how to do it on my own.

Sam is the best friend anyone could have. He's like an angel from another world, and as he held my arm while we walked away, he was reading my heart, guiding me.

"I'll help you," he spelled on my hand, "but you're going to have to tell me everything."

❧ Thirty-One ❧

I took Sam to the shed.

"What's this?" Sam asked.

It was Dad's guitar, zipped up in a canvas guitar-shaped bag.

"Dad doesn't play anymore," I tapped. "He said it's broken."

Sam opened the zipper and ran his fingers along the strings, leaning his left ear near. And then he found what was wrong: in the bottom of the bag was the guitar pick for strumming the guitar, snapped in two pieces like a broken heart.

I pinned up a photograph of Mom holding me when I was a baby, looking at me, laughing, loving.

I pinned it next to the new photograph of Homeless.

Then I told Sam. Sometimes you had to explain things to Sam that he had never heard of before. Sometimes he seemed to know things with his own secret brilliant heart and understanding.

"What do you think is out there?" I spelled.

"Clothesline," Sam tapped.

"No, out there, in space."

Sam frowned. "What, like heaven?" he tapped.

"Maybe."

"You must have an idea, or you wouldn't ask me."

I liked what Sam spelled; it just showed how clever he was.

He closed his eyes and spread his arms out. He found my face and put his hand over my eyes. I heard sounds: faraway footsteps, faraway cars, faraway birds. I heard all the everyday things, and they made me feel safe.

"Sometimes I wonder if the stars are people," I spelled.

"What sort of people?"

"People who used to be on earth."

I thought that heaven was up there somewhere—that's what people said—but maybe the distant stars were the people gone from earth. Maybe that was what a ghost was, one of our stars come to visit us.

"What are stars like?" Sam tapped.

"If there were no stars, it would just be completely black."

That's probably what it was like for Sam being blind. Like there were no stars in the night sky, no moon, no streetlights, no flashlights.

"There's no noise up there either," I spelled, "nothing. All we have is the stars, and they make you feel you're not alone."

Sam smiled.

"Are you a star?" he tapped.

"Not me. I'm not the star."

"Who then?"

There was no going back. "My mom," I spelled. "She died last year."

Sam went quiet for a minute, so still.

"Why would she go so far away?" he tapped.

Maybe it was because of what Sam spelled, I don't know, but it felt as if she were right there in the shed, right next to me.

"Maybe she didn't," I tapped.

Sam didn't say anything. He was leaning up on his elbow, grinning.

"Why are you laughing?" I tapped.

And suddenly I wasn't going to tell him. He was going to laugh at me, say it wasn't true, and I felt stupid that I was going to trust him. He might be blind and deaf, but he was just like all the others. I pushed his hand away.

He wiped his hand over his mouth, wiped the grin away, grabbed my hand back.

"Not laughing, happy. What's the matter?" he spelled, holding my hand tight.

"You're just like all the others," I spelled. "They think I can't see her, but I can."

Sam sat cross-legged with his head drooping, and I sat with my back to him. Of all people it was stupid to have told Sam. How could he believe what he couldn't see?

When I turned around, there was a gentle smile on Sam's moon-colored face.

"Can anyone else see her?" he spelled slowly.

And that's when I knew what I had to do.

"I think Jed can," I spelled.

❧ Thirty-Two ❧

On my bed there was a really old silver tape recorder, one that Dad used to play music on when he was young. The little note stuck to it said, "Play me."

"This is your dad speaking. . . . This is a message for Cally," it said. Then a sigh and shuffled paper. "You can say anything you like into this recorder. And if you want, you can let anyone you like listen to it. But if you want to record something and don't want anyone to listen to it, then that's all right too." It went quiet again. "That's it for now. Over and out."

I pressed it to my ear and played it again. The

same words. The same message.

Dad came in.

"Your burger's getting cold," he said.

He put the plate on my bed.

"Did you listen to it?" he said, picking up the tape recorder.

He played it back, heard the soft crackle of no reply after his message. He tapped the button, rewound. He sighed.

"Dr. Colborn's idea, you know, the expert," he said, holding up the recorder. "She wrote me a letter."

What did she know? She was just going to make everything worse.

I stared through the wet window. I wondered what Dad would say if Jed said he could see Mom too. Would he believe Jed? Would he see that Homeless belonged with us?

"Hello-oh," Dad said with the recorder at his mouth, "is there anybody there?"

He played it back. Then he spoke into it again.

"Hello, yes, this is Cally's dad. I'm sitting on Cally's bed at the moment, which, even though it's dinnertime, still hasn't been made."

He sighed again, left the machine on Record.

"Cally won't tell me what color she wants her bedroom painted, so I'm going to have to guess. She didn't look too excited when I suggested pink." He lay down on the bed, smiling. "So I'm guessing maybe brown or possibly gray."

He lifted his head, saw my folded arms and frowning face.

"Maybe not," he saïd into the recorder, lying flat again.

He sat up, dragged one of the boxes over, and peeled back the lid.

"She still hasn't unpacked any of her things either, although her dirty clothes are all over the floor."

He pulled things from the box.

"So what have we got here? Books . . ." He placed them on my bed. "You need to sort these books out; some of them are baby books. You don't read these anymore."

He pulled out more things.

"Smelly shoes"—he went on—"boxes of beads for losing down the back of the sofa, necklaces, old jeans, old felt tips."

He emptied everything onto my bed.

"Come on, Cally, it's about time you sorted this stuff out and put it away or threw it away. You were supposed to do that before we moved. We've been here weeks now, and we're staying put, you know that. You can't live out of boxes forever."

He sighed again.

"What am I going to do with you?"

Hadn't I tried to tell him a thousand times? If he would just let her still be here with us, just say, "Remember when your mom said . . ." and bring her back with words.

He found a picture sticking out from under the bed, the one me and Mom had drawn of each other. We held it between us. He left the recorder running.

"You know what she'd say right now?" his heart couldn't help saying.

She used to say it all the time when Dad moaned or argued and went on and on about work and boring stuff. I remembered her rolling her eyes and pulling faces at him. I remembered her giving him a hug. And she said it in my heart just as Dad said it:

"Play us a tune or sing us a song, but for heaven's sake, stop going on."

And sometimes he would. Well, he used to. He'd get his guitar out, sing a song, or just play a tune. Sometimes me and Mom sang with him.

Dad laughed softly. He looked into my eyes.

"That's what she'd say," he said.

We stared into the drawing, as if we could still see her hand holding the pencil. For a minute he looked like he really remembered her, like he knew the winter was over.

"I wish your mother were here right now," he said. "She'd know what to do about you."

❧ Thirty-Three ❧

More rain gushed down the windows, filled up the drains, and made great puddles and ponds in the road and on the common. Mrs. Cooper said, "Absolutely not in this weather," when Sam asked if we could go to the common. We wanted to find Homeless and make sure he was safe; find Jed and ask him, somehow, about Mom.

"I don't ever remember so much rain," Mrs. Cooper said, looking into the sky, "not this time of year. The river in town will burst its banks if it goes on like this. And besides, you can't go out; you've got another hospital appointment later, Sam."

We sat together on the window seat, played hand-clapping games.

"What is a ghost?" Sam tapped on my hand.

"A dead person come back," I spelled.

"Can you touch them or smell them?"

"No, you can only see them. But you can sort of hear them, like a—"

I realized Sam wouldn't understand TV because he couldn't hear or see one. The Coopers didn't even have a television set.

"You know what a telephone is?" I spelled.

Sam smiled and put his hand by his ear, pretended he was holding one. He explained he could tell when the telephone was ringing. They had a telephone with really big numbers. It rang like a bell and buzzed so Sam could feel the vibrations. He spelled that sometimes his mom gave him messages from people who called up.

"A bit like that," I tapped.

You can tell when Sam is trying to work things out or remember something. He hangs his head; his long black bangs fall over his face. The only thing that moves is his bony thin chest, and you can just hear a little wheeze at the end of his quick breathing.

"Like a message," he spelled.

He leaned back.

"Can you phone them?" he tapped.

Sam isn't like ordinary people. He thinks about things differently. Maybe it's because he can't see or hear, but sometimes what he says just makes me feel like my brain and heart are exploding. In a good way. I wanted to tell him he was magic because he made me feel like I wasn't weird or crazy or stupid.

All the time I had been waiting for Mom to come, like the day she died. Me and Luke waited and waited after school for her to come home and cook our supper. The house still smelled of the pancakes we'd had for Dad's birthday that morning; his birthday cake was on the kitchen table, but Mom hadn't iced or decorated it. She must have forgotten something, because she'd driven the car out of town. She was coming back, but . . . there was a crash.

Sam put his ear against the window. His fingers crawled along the wooden bits, gently searching. He found a tiny moth with shivering wings pulling itself from a thin cocoon. It had a thin red stripe and ragged red spots on its black wings. Sam nudged it, and it stepped onto his finger. He made a cage with his fingers and caught it in his hand.

He held it out and put it on my hand. The moth spread its wings over my palm. Underneath the wings were vivid red.

"Phone your mom," Sam spelled, "just like on a telephone."

I thought about Mom; I thought about her really hard. I made a cage with my fingers around the red moth, I closed my eyes. I could still see the brilliant red of the moth's wings; they spread and changed into a different shape. A red coat.

And she was there, right inside me.

Mom, I said in my heart, *Sam's magic, isn't he?*

Oh, yes, she said, *and so are you.*

Are you a ghost, Mom? I asked her silently in my mind.

I don't think so. Ghosts are spooky, scary things, aren't they?

I suppose. But I told people . . . well, I told them you're a ghost. It doesn't matter, because they don't believe me anyway. Are you an angel or a star then?

She laughed. *Me? An angel? A star? I'm your mom, Cally.*

I know that, but—

Her voice was suddenly serious. *Now I want you to listen very carefully.*

She seemed brighter than ever, as if there were a spotlight on her, but she was also quivering and blurred.

Remember the clock inside the big old cathedral, the way they painted the solar system?

I thought about that not very long ago.

They painted the earth in the middle; and the sun went around the outside, and I said—

People get things the wrong way around. I remember.

She smiled. *Exactly.*

I don't get it.

Well, what you think is on the outside is in the middle.

Like your name is my middle name.

Just like that.

I felt her in the middle of me. That's when I noticed my belly didn't hurt anymore. I'd gotten so used to aching.

I thought you were up in space or something.

Why would I go so far away? Just because you can't see me it doesn't mean I'm not here with you.

That's what Sam said.

She seemed to be evaporating, the redness of her coat like dying fire.

But I did see you, I said in my heart.

And what if you can't?

I couldn't look away from her, burning brightly in the middle of my mind. That's when I knew she would go away soon and I would never see her in the world again.

What about Homeless? I whispered silently, trying hard not to cry. *Is he going away too?*

Things return where they belong, she said.

The moth slipped between my fingers. It circled around the ceiling, flashing red and black in the shadows of the dark corners.

Sam opened the window, and like a tiny flame, the moth fluttered away.

"You phoned," said Sam, grinning.

He knew. I wanted to ask him how, but he'd stopped smiling and said, "Hospital now. I hate hospitals."

❧ Thirty-Four ❧

Mrs. Brooks and Miss Steadman stopped talking when me and Dad arrived at Mrs. Brooks's office.

"How nice to see you again, Mr. Fisher," she said, shaking his hand, but her smile wasn't a real one. "This is just a short meeting so that we are all up to speed on what's happening."

"Good," he said. "I have to get back to work."

Dad sat down, crossed his legs, and folded his arms.

"We've had the doctor's report and have passed it on to Dr. Colborn along with our own report," said Mrs. Brooks. Her eyelashes fluttered as she looked down at some papers. "I understand she wrote directly to you."

"She did. She suggested I use a tape recorder."

"And how's that going?"

Dad didn't look at me. If he had, he might have worked out that I was thinking that maybe he ought to see Dr. Colborn instead.

"I'm not sure a tape recorder is the answer."

"I see," Mrs. Brooks said, taking her glasses off her head and polishing them. "And nothing else seems to be working?"

They talk like you're not there. Discussing the best way forward, useful suggestions, long-term strategies.

"Well, Dr. Colborn has asked to come into school and see Cally. She's made an appointment for next week," said Mrs. Brooks.

Just knowing she was coming made my stomach turn.

"We just want you to know we are all doing our best to sort this out."

Dad coughed like he had something stuck in his throat.

"Well, that's all, really. Anything you'd like to

say, Miss Steadman?"

She shook her head, then said, "No, but I have a message from Mr. Crisp. He still hopes Cally will sing at the end-of-term concert."

Dad closed his eyes, turned his face to the ceiling. He opened his eyes, faced me, and I could see his disappointment. He shook his head.

"Oh, Cally," he said softly.

Mrs. Brooks thanked Dad for coming in and said she'd stay in touch.

"There's just one other thing, Mr. Fisher," she said, getting up. "We've been having some problems with a very large dog coming onto the school grounds."

"A gray wolfhound-type dog?" Dad said, his eyes wide while he glared at me.

"Yes, that's it. Cally was with it on the playing field a few weeks ago. It turned up at concert practice after school a couple of times. Its howling outside the hall is very disturbing for the children. I'm afraid we haven't been able to apprehend the creature; it just seems to come and go as it pleases."

I remembered reading about dogs in the library that the reason they howled was so they could talk to their families, even the ones that had gone, even the ones a long, long way away.

Dad put his hand over his eyes and sighed.

"Can you shed any light on this matter?" Mrs. Brooks asked, perching her glasses back on her head. "Does the dog belong to you?"

"No," Dad said, "it definitely doesn't belong to us."

"Well, we have called the local authority," said Mrs. Brooks. "The dog warden is coming during the next concert practice."

❧ Thirty-Five ❧

The list of times for concert practice was stuck on the music-room door with the names of the children who had to be there. After school I stood at the back next to where the big glass doors of the assembly hall were open and the long blackout curtains puffed in the breeze. I know Mr. Crisp saw me, and I pretended to sing, opening and closing my mouth, while they all practiced the big finale song. Mr. Crisp's mouth twitched from side to side, but he didn't say anything.

Mia and Daisy saw me too. Mia kept twisting around to look at me, whispering to Daisy.

She put her hand up when they stopped singing.

"Yes, Mia," said Mr. Crisp.

"Cally Fisher's at the back, and she's not even in the concert."

A ripple went through the children as they all turned to look at me.

"Thank you—" started Mr. Crisp.

Daisy continued. "She didn't put her name down like you're supposed to. And she's been bringing a dog to school and you're not allowed."

"I don't think—"

"And my mom said when she finds out who messed up my shoes—"

"That's enough," said Mr. Crisp. "Concert practice is for singing, not telling tales. Everyone, eyes this way."

Just then we all heard a sad *how-how-howool*.

Daisy's hand shot up again, and by now her voice was screechy.

"See, I told you, they're coming to take it away before it hurts somebody."

I slipped out between the billowing curtains, saw Homeless, his head up high, howling. He greeted me, swish-swishing his tail and weaving around me. *Hush,* I said silently. *Don't let them know you're here.*

Then I saw Mrs. Brooks through her office window, heard her bang on the glass. But I didn't care. Homeless was beside me, close against me, telling me with his soft eyes just like I was telling him: we were supposed to be together. And because he was with me, I thought he would be safe.

I ran, with Homeless by my side, across the playing field, heading for somewhere far away from everyone. But before we could get to the gate, a van pulled up on the drive, and a man and a lady jumped out and ran toward us. They had long sticks with loops around the end, but Homeless danced about too far away for them to reach.

Mrs. Brooks shouted, "Cally, come away from the dog."

Children were piling out through the hall doors. Daisy started shrieking. Mr. Crisp was trying to herd everyone back inside. The shrieking went on.

The man and lady were throwing dog treats toward Homeless.

"Come here," said the dog warden. "There's a good boy."

Homeless must have been hungry, because he stopped running and looked toward the biscuits scattered in the grass.

"Cally," Mrs. Brooks puffed, running toward me, "I want you to come over here. Now, please."

I should have made sure he had food so he wasn't hungry. I shouldn't have looked at Mrs. Brooks. I shouldn't have taken my eyes off Homeless. She stopped me from running away with him.

I saw the loop slip over his head and around his neck. I saw the sadness in his face when he found he couldn't come to me with two of them holding the end of the stick.

❧ Thirty-Six ❧

I didn't think anyone would find me.

Sam was with Jed when they knocked on the shed door.

"Jed's here. He's okay, but he can't find Homeless," Sam tapped.

I spelled out what had happened at school.

Sam went back into his apartment to collect some cards from his boxes to tell Jed.

Jed turned around and around slowly, looking up and down at the pictures I had drawn and the photographs pinned on the shed walls. There were photos of Homeless, of me and Luke as babies, in our school uniforms with brushed hair and gappy teeth, family vacations, birthdays and Christmas mornings, Mom and Dad on their wedding day. Hundreds of smiling faces. All the best days of our lives together.

Jed's eyes crinkled. He peered closer at one photograph, of all four of us, the only one with Mom in her red raincoat.

He touched the picture. My heart leaped.

"Your mom?"

My heart felt like it would explode, beating faster and faster.

He stared at the pictures. He looked into my eyes and nodded to himself.

"You've got her eyes," he said.

The door crashed against the side of the shed as Sam came stumbling back in a hurry, wheezing. He spelled on my hand that he had asked his mom what you had to do to get a dog back from the dog pound, and she said you have to prove it's your dog and pay about a hundred dollars. He said he didn't tell her why he was asking, but she guessed it was Jed's dog and said perhaps it was best to leave him with people who could find him a good home.

Sam gave some cards to Jed: BIG, DOG, GONE, VAN, and MONEY.

Jed's eyes glistened with tears. Then he wiped them and smiled.

"We've got to get him back."

❧ Thirty-Seven ❧

The next day I had to see the evil witch, Dr. Colborn. My hands felt cold. I squashed myself against the wall and squeezed my lips together when I saw her coming along the hall with Mrs. Brooks. Everything about Dr. Colborn was small, like she was the minimum a person could be. Tiny blue eyes, small freckled face, very short grayish hair. Her light-colored skirt and jacket fitted her exactly.

Mrs. Brooks said, "This is Cally Fisher," and gave me a see-where-all-this-has-got-you look. They looked funny standing next to each other, tall and small.

"Would you like me to sit in?" Mrs. Brooks asked,

her orange lips thin with her smile.

"No," said Dr. Colborn. "I have your report."

"Oh," said Mrs. Brooks. "Would you like some coffee or something?"

"No," said the doctor.

She didn't even say no, thank you. She just sat down in Mrs. Brooks's chair, stood up, and took the pink cushion off and handed it to Mrs. Brooks without saying anything else.

"I'll leave you to it then," Mrs. Brooks said, looking for somewhere else to put the cushion. "I'll be next door if you want anything."

Dr. Colborn pulled some papers out of her leather bag. I saw my name on a thin file. She put it on the table and didn't open it.

"Before we do anything else, I need to tell you something," she said, sitting up straight. She spoke very fast. "I never take any notice of the things people tell me about someone I've never met. Good or bad, none of it. Nod if you understand."

I did. She hardly waited before she went on.

"So that means I know nothing about you and you also know nothing about me. Does that sound like a good place to start? Nod if you understand."

She spoke quickly, but I couldn't tell if she was happy or irritated or anything. I nodded.

"Secondly, I don't mind if you already have ideas about what we are going to do in our time together. Maybe you think I'm going to be mean or make you do something you don't want to. . . . Am I going too fast? Nod or shake your head."

I shook my head. She didn't stop there.

"I find it a lot easier, and much more satisfying, I have to say, to find out things for myself. Yes? Otherwise we're all in a muddle even before we start, aren't we?"

All of a sudden it was quite funny. She spoke really quickly; and like a ninny, I just sat there trying to keep up with my head nodding and shaking. I couldn't help it. I laughed. Dr. Colborn leaned back, crossed her legs, and laughed too.

"So, now you can see something of what I'm like," she said.

We laughed.

"And I can see a little bit of what you're like. And thank goodness you seem. quite, quite normal." She winked. "Only the very strange ones don't laugh at me."

I was still smiling.

"Actually, nobody has ever not laughed at me," she said. She patted the file. "Shall we get the boring facts out of the way?"

I nodded before she had chance to say, "Nod if you understand."

She opened the file, flicked through some papers, closed it again.

"Doctor says you're fit and healthy. Teachers, family, friends say you don't speak. Does that sound like a reasonable summary of the situation?"

Nodding.

"And I have also been informed that you can speak and sing very well."

Her voice had slowed, and she looked at me for a long time.

"I'm very sorry about your mom."

She never took her eyes off me.

"I would like to ask you a question. You can nod or shake your head, that's fine. The question is: Are you going to speak again?"

When someone asks you something like that out of the blue, it's hard to think of an answer. So I shrugged.

Then the break time bell rang.

Dr. Colborn unbuttoned her neat jacket and went to look out the window. Children went out through the doors, chatting and screaming, laughing and yelling in the playground.

And then, believe it or not, we just stood there for the whole of the break time. Just looking out the window. We watched football games and chasing games. We saw someone scrape his knees trying to escape, heard screams from someone in tears. We heard arguing over a ball. We saw third-grade girls skipping along, linked in a chain, singing. And then the whistle and all the voices settled to a murmur and the doors closed behind the last children who went in.

Dr. Colborn said, "Where would we be without our voices?" But that was all.

We sat down, and she started talking quite fast again, telling me about some of the things she did with children who had trouble talking to help them not be scared of their own voices and what people might think about what they said.

"But I have a funny feeling none of that is going to work for you. And you know why?"

I shook my head.

"Because you shrugged when I asked if you were going to speak again."

I felt my mouth open and closed it.

"You see," she said, picking up speed, "if you'd shaken your head, meaning no, then that would have meant I had to help you. And you wouldn't want that, would you?"

She smiled.

"If you'd nodded, that might have meant one of two things. Either you were just saying yes to keep me happy, or you were waiting for a particular thing to happen."

She stopped talking and breathed a deep breath.

"Do you know, Cally, that people communicate with their bodies all the time? Tiny little vibrations and movements all tell a story about someone. Their eyes give them away. Can I ask you something else?"

I thought she could see right inside me, right into my heart. And I didn't mind. I could tell she was really nice.

"Until the thing happens that you're waiting for, do you have someone like a friend or teddy bear or

a pet"—she leaned forward and whispered—
"someone you can talk to, even if it's not out loud?"

I didn't nod, but I couldn't stop my eyes from fill-
ing up. I kept blinking and then wondered what
she'd think that meant.

She looked me straight in the eye and said,
"Good. I'm very glad."

She put my file in her bag, buttoned her jacket,
and stood up.

"Most people think that they should have what
they want, just like that." She snapped her fingers.
"They don't want to wait; they're impatient and
don't understand that everything takes its own
time. Change happens when things are ready.
Understand?"

She went to shake my hand but squeezed it
instead and said, "I wanted to get to know you
today. And I'm very happy to have met you."

I thought that too.

"I'll come back and see you next week, see what
I can do to help," she said. "In the meantime, I
think whatever reason you have for not communi-
cating must be very, very important to you."

❧ Thirty-Eight ❧

Mrs. Cooper and Sam were waiting for me when I got home. They showed me the note pushed under the door. It was in Jed's nice, tidy writing.

It said: COME TO THE MUSIC SHOP, TODAY, FROM JED.

"Sam's not told me exactly what's going on," said Mrs. Cooper. "But he says we must go. And I gather that you'll want to come too."

I nodded madly, tapping on Sam's hand, "What's it about?"

Sam put his hand over his heart, patted his chest. "Good feeling," he said.

Mrs. Cooper phoned Dad, asked if I could go into town with them on the bus. She winked while she was talking, but she didn't say why we were going. Dad said okay, as long as I was not back too late.

After a short walk from the bus stop I could already see there were people gathered around The Music Shop. There was a man juggling with forks and spoons. He was wearing a checked shirt with the sleeves rolled up and a nice pair of blue trousers. His beard was gone, and his hair cut short, but the sparkling eyes told me it was Jed.

At his feet there was an orange woolly hat and a sign saying HOMELESS.

People clapped as more and more spoons flew through the air. The forks clinked when they passed in his hands. His face was completely concentrated on what he was doing.

Jed caught the forks and spoons, made a small bow, put his hands together like a prayer when people clapped and sprinkled coins in his hat.

"I didn't recognize you," said Mrs. Cooper as the shoppers went on their way.

Jed ruffled Sam's hair and let Sam feel around

his face. Sam smiled and tapped on his mom's hand, and she said, "Sam says you're very smart."

Mrs. Cooper looked at the coins spilling on the pavement. You could tell she was working things out. She offered to count the money for Jed.

Just then Luke came over. He was with Rachel, and she said, "We saw the note. What are you up to? Can we join in?"

Mrs. Cooper was holding all the money in her hands, chewing her lip.

"This is to get the dog back, isn't it?" she said.

"Do you have enough?" asked Rachel, straightening her hair band.

Jed smiled at her. "Can you juggle?" he said.

"No," she said, and then her eyes became wide and excited. "Be back in a minute."

She rushed into The Music Shop, and we saw her through the window talking to the man inside.

Rachel came out waving a drum over her head.

"He let me borrow it." She laughed. "And I can make music."

There was something about the way Rachel drummed. The sound was like a magnet, like when the Pied Piper made all the children follow him.

More and more people couldn't help coming over to listen to her drumming, to watch the flash of silver from the forks and spoons flying through Jed's hands. Sam held my hand the whole time. He didn't move, not a tiny bit. My heart fell in with the sound and was part of the music too, part of Sam, part of everything. Rachel made us dance on the inside.

Soon the money was clinking in Jed's hat again. The clapping was louder; people stayed longer.

When the shops shut and people started to go home, Mrs. Cooper counted the money again. I saw her add some money from her purse.

She handed it all back to Jed and smiled. "You should have enough now."

I saw the brightness in Jed's eyes. He turned to look at me.

"I'll bring him home," he said, "where he's meant to be."

❧ Thirty-Nine ❧

S am and me sat on the wall outside. The street was dark, but even though it was late in the evening, the sky was still light.

"You have to persuade your dad when Jed gets back with Homeless," Sam spelled.

"He doesn't believe me."

"You have to make him."

"How?"

"You have to speak to him," Sam spelled. "Tell him why Homeless means so much to you."

Sam got his inhaler out of his pocket. "You want Homeless, don't you?"

More than anything, I wanted Homeless to come and live with us, make us a family of four again.

Sam shuffled along the wall, leaned against me. "What's a song like?" he spelled.

Sometimes Sam made me feel like I was really clever and he was asking me because he thought I knew the answer. Mr. Crisp knew all about music and singing. So did my mom.

"It starts down here," I spelled, patting my hands on his skinny middle. It tickled, and he laughed. "It starts with your breath—"

I saw the sadness fall on Sam's face.

And I was going to tell him about listening and hearing, but that would have left Sam out. And Mom said singing didn't do that, leave people out. It knitted people together.

"It's a gift," I spelled. "It's something that you give."

I heard a blackbird whistling. *Hear the sweet blackbird,* she whispered. *Hear it sing that it's safe to sleep and dream.* I knew Sam couldn't hear Mom but wondered if he could feel her somewhere deep inside, like I did.

"It's something my mom gave me."

"Your mom's nice," he spelled. "I can tell. I can feel it, like she's here with you now." He held my hand. And I knew how special his skin was, how big his heart was. "I believe you," he said.

"Your mom's nice too," I spelled.

Sam breathed in the inhaler.

"She thinks I'm still a baby. She won't let me do what I want."

"What do you want to do?"

Sam shrugged, hung his head and shoulders; his long bangs fell over his face. Then he sat up, tried to take another deep breath, held it with his chest up high. He coughed and spluttered, threw the inhaler down.

"What's wrong?" I spelled. I'd never seen him like this before.

He put my hand on his chest over his heart. I leaned over, rested my ear there, listened to the strange liquid beat.

He smiled a bit; then he spelled, "It doesn't work properly."

I thought about Sam's heart. To me he had the best heart anyone could have, a mysterious heart that told him things I only dreamed of.

"I don't want another operation."

He pulled down the neck of his T-shirt, showed

me the fat pink scar snaking down along the middle of his chest.

I remembered the sticker on Sam's calendar, the important date.

"It's soon, isn't it?" I tapped.

He nodded once.

"Mom gets scared," he spelled.

I could have told Sam he was being selfish. I didn't even have a mom anymore. And when I felt a little stab in my heart, I nearly wanted to argue with him. But something made me think differently. I remembered the mouse Sam had shown me in his mind, so tiny but so brave inside, and knew he wasn't talking about his mom.

"Don't be scared," I spelled. "I'll be with you always. You're my best friend."

Tears rolled down his moon-colored face, and he wiped them with his shoulder.

"Take me swimming," he spelled. "You and me."

I sensed the water, its waves spilling around, soft and cool, holding us up, speaking of watery things to us through the whole of our skin.

"I will," I tapped. "Before your operation I'll take you, and we'll swim together."

❦ *Forty* ❧

For the next couple of days it rained like
waterfalls. Sam and me waited, but there
was no sign of Jed or Homeless. Sam
crossed the days off his calendar, and I saw the
sticker get closer and closer.

We waited with the front door wide open, holding the big umbrella from the shed, until Mrs.
Cooper made us come in because there was a
puddle in the hall. We waited in the shed, and I
looked at all the walls with every photograph and
picture we had and remembered everything, heard
us speaking and laughing and singing as if the pictures were TV screens. I drew another picture, of

how I'd like things to be. I drew me, Luke, and Dad and was just about to draw Homeless with a long, long red leash for us all to hold, when I heard something, heard someone coming through the front door.

And then it was like a car crash, a pileup of people.

Me and Sam came running through the back door. Luke was there in the passageway holding Homeless by a new collar.

"I found him outside," he said, wiping the rain from his face. "You're in big trouble now, Cally. You know Dad's already said we can't keep him."

Mrs. Cooper was just coming out of their apartment doorway with the box of cooking equipment that I'd left there. She tripped over Sam's blue swimming bag, which was on the floor in the way as usual, and the set of red bowls tumbled and clanked around the floor. Sam was apologizing when Dad came in through the front door.

You could see Mrs. Cooper felt awkward having the box of Mom's old things. She opened her mouth to speak, but Dad exploded.

"Just because we share the same building and

yard doesn't mean you're entitled to things that belong to me!" he said, gritting his teeth and staring hard at the box.

Mrs. Cooper's mouth hung open as she tried to get out her reply.

"It's not what you think. I was just—" she started to say.

"And what's that dog doing here, Luke? I thought I made it clear!" Dad snapped.

"It wasn't me," Luke said. "I just found him outside."

Luke let go of his collar, and Homeless rushed to me, greeted me, wound around me and Sam.

"Dad, it wasn't me. Tell him, Cally," said Luke.

"I didn't know the dog was here either," said Mrs. Cooper.

Then we all heard Jed's quiet, husky voice. "I brought him here."

"And who are you?" asked Dad, spinning around with the rest of us to see Jed in the doorway, his arms full of shopping bags, stuffed with everything he owned.

"This is Jed," said Mrs. Cooper. "I thought he was Jed's dog."

Jed shook his head. "I've just been looking after him until I could bring him home."

Dad's eyes flashed.

"Home?" Dad snapped. His voice was all high-pitched. "Home? This isn't the dog's home."

Now he looked even angrier with Mrs. Cooper as well, because she seemed to know more about what was going on than he did. Jed came over to me, looked at me with his starry eyes.

Dad's eyes narrowed; he pushed in front of me and stood close to Jed.

"Look, I don't know who you are, but you're very much mistaken. This is not our dog!"

"Oh, he is," said Jed. "I'm sure of that."

We all followed Jed to the shed. Dad stopped suddenly and looked around at all the walls, at all the family photographs, the drawings of Homeless and Mom. Jed took a photo off the wall, the only one with Mom in her red raincoat next to Dad, Luke, and me, standing in front of the big old cathedral. He held the photo out to Dad, spoke softly.

"This is the lady who gave me the dog. I found her . . . after the car accident . . . I tried to help."

He stopped a moment as Homeless padded into the shed.

"She had a puppy in the car with her." Jed smoothed Homeless's head. "He was the puppy."

I grabbed Dad's hand, to hold on to him while my heart burst open. Homeless was ours. He really had always been ours.

"The ambulance and police came . . . they made me go. She asked me to take the puppy with me, to find you."

Dad put his hand over his mouth, closed his eyes. I watched the silent tear on his cheek.

"She said you would need him . . . we all would. I didn't know who you were, but she made me promise to bring him home. I've been looking for you for more than a year."

Dad's hand was tight around mine, as if he were holding on too. When someone tells you the truth like that, all your skin and bones and insides know. We were all waiting for Dad to speak, to say something.

Jed continued. "I saw Cally in town one day, saw her eyes just like her mom's, and that's how I knew I'd found you."

But Dad's hand slipped from mine as he turned away, touched the pictures on the wall, held his fingers on their wedding photograph.

"Dad?" said Luke from behind us.

Dad's voice quavered. He turned to Jed.

"How do we know you're telling the truth, that this isn't some story from Cally's vivid imagination, some story she's convinced you about?"

Jed pulled himself up straight and looked Dad in the eye. "Because Cally's never said a word to me. Not one."

❧ Forty-One ❧

Dad turned away from us all again and folded his arms tight around himself. It seemed as if he had left us too and couldn't come back to us anymore. No matter what anyone said. Didn't he believe Jed? Why wasn't he saying anything? The silence was so painful.

And I wanted Sam, to tell him so he would know what to do now, so he could tell me something that would make me think differently. That's when I noticed he wasn't there. Why wasn't he there?

I ran down the passageway, went to their open apartment door. Sam's swimming bag was missing. I saw the front door open, the front gate wide. The sunflowers were bending down from the weight of all the rain. I ran across the road. The puddles on the common had turned dark gray, just like the sky. There was a figure in a red raincoat in the distance, far across the common, and she was calling me, telling me to come, telling me to find Sam.

The rain fell down, sprayed up as I ran. I couldn't see Sam, but I knew where he was. I knew that even though he was blind, he would find his way to Swan Lake. Every time we'd gone there, he'd felt all the trees and lumps and bumps in the ground, mapped the common in his mind. When we'd pushed the stroller, he'd seemed to know where we were going. I ran faster than I'd ever run before. My chest hurt; my eyes stung from the cold rain. I didn't stop until I saw the gates and scrabbled through the hole in the bricks.

I saw the pile of clothes and the empty swimming bag. I saw the lake trembling with hissing rain. The lake was much bigger than before, flooded right up to the steps by the old ticket office, swamping the bushes and trees. Streams of cloudy water ran down the clay banks, swirling around the edge as the level of the water crept up the sides.

I saw his white, skinny body in his swimming trunks and the blue band of the goggles around the back of his head. He was almost up to his waist in the black water. I saw him lean in, and under he went.

I kicked off my shoes, ran through the cold water, swam through twigs and leaves, newspaper and rubbish, all the loose things that had been swept into the lake. The rain pelted the surface, and I couldn't see clearly.

Sam came up again farther ahead; I heard as he kicked and coughed and splashed. Then I couldn't see him at all, until his arms and head broke through the surface. He went under again. I swam harder and harder and reached the broken stump still sticking out of the water. The black water swirled with white clouds from the clay. I held my breath; I thought of him; I reached down. I found his hand, he caught mine, and I dragged him up again. I put my arms around his chest and heaved him over to the stump, and we held on with our arms around the trunk. He spluttered and choked. His arms were covered in goose bumps, his short breath wheezed, he shivered, and his teeth chattered. Sam's hand ran over my face, so he knew who I was. A piece of string was caught around his arm.

The rain clattered on the surface. I didn't think Sam could swim back. He looked weak, and his narrow chest was going in and out fast. His face was pale, and his lips had turned blue. I didn't think I was strong enough to swim back holding him up. Then Sam's eyes closed; he seemed to lose his grip; he went heavy in my arms.

Mom, I said silently, *I don't know what to do.*

I saw her. She was in her red raincoat and green rain hat, dressed for a rainy day. She was standing on the steps by the ticket office, the water running over her feet. I heard her in my heart: *Yes, you do.*

But I need you, I said silently, my eyes stinging hot from tears.

Mom's silent voice was full of warmth. *Just call,* she said. *He'll find you.*

I remembered what she'd said before about Homeless: *One day he'll find you.*

I felt Sam's feeble fingers trying to tap a message on my hand, but I couldn't feel what he was saying. The only thing I could think was that if I spoke, if

185

I called, it would be the end; Mom would go away forever. And Homeless didn't know his name; I'd never spoken his name to him. How would he hear me? How would he know it was me?

Sam took my hand. "She's here now, isn't she?" he spelled.

I put his hand on my cheek and nodded. Mom faded, the red of her raincoat evaporating. Sam quaked and was ghostly pale.

I took a deep breath. I was really frightened now for Sam. So I opened my mouth to call for help. But nothing came out. My voice wasn't working. I didn't even know what I was going to shout. I tried again. Nothing but choking on the water leaping off the surface.

Sam took my hand and spelled out three letters. He put his thumb and finger on either end of my pointing finger, touched my thumb, then put his thumb and finger on either end of my pointing finger again. Then his head fell forward. I could hardly see his chest move or hear him breathe.

I filled my ribs and belly with air, felt the tightness, fit to burst. I shouted at the top of my voice what Sam had spelled, what I knew I had to say.

"DAD!"

Through the thundering sheets of rain, Homeless appeared by the ticket office. Mom burned again brightly. He ran straight into the water toward us. His paws made big long paddles. I hooked one of Sam's arms over his neck and the other around mine, and together we tried to swim back. We weren't strong enough. Now I couldn't breathe with the water going in my mouth, and Homeless was struggling, reaching his head up as high as he could.

"DAD!" I cried.

And Dad was there. Holding Sam up, holding me up, letting Homeless free to swim back by himself. We climbed onto the ticket office ledge.

"Can you run with me?" Dad asked, scooping Sam in his arms.

Mom was still there, watching, with such love and hope in her eyes. She put her hand in her pocket. She reached out as Dad ran past her, as if she were going to touch him.

The long piece of string hung from Sam's limp

arm. The crumbling model wooden boat dragged out of the water and trailed behind us as we ran back across the common. Dad looked back only once to see Homeless was with me and we were coming as fast as we could.

❧Forty-Two❧

The doctor standing at the bottom of the bed said, "We'll need to keep her in the hospital overnight, just as a precaution."

He left me under the strange orange glow of a lamp, with Dad sitting next to my bed.

"Can we talk?" he said.

It was thirty-one days since we'd talked together. Maybe it was much longer than that. It depends on what you think talking is. It's not just words. It's much more than that, much, much more. And I told him everything, my story. And he did what he always used to do. He listened, with all of him.

Dad was holding a photograph. Four smiling

faces: me, Mom, Dad, and Luke, standing on the green grass outside the cathedral, Mom in her red raincoat, her arms spread out and along our backs, the cathedral yellow with the sun on it.

And then I knew. If she wasn't here to tell us, to show us we could still shine, then it was as if we were nothing. But all we had to do was remember.

"Dad, we don't have to talk about every Christmas and birthday. I just want you to talk about her, because when you do, I remember her. As if she were here."

"I know," he said.

"Dad, we could just talk a little bit, like you did with my homework, and then keep practicing until we can do it easily."

He laughed. "Does that mean you're going to try harder with your math?"

"No. It means we need to do it together."

And then he talked. We looked at the photograph, and he talked about the cathedral, about the worn stone steps going up to the tower, how soft the stones seemed, how they led up through archways, leading higher and higher. Then he smiled. And he didn't say anything about her. But we could see her on the steps, looking over her shoulder, seeing nobody else was around, and then singing "Stairway to Heaven" to us.

Dad looked into my eyes.

"She bought the puppy for you because she loved to hear you sing. Did you know that?"

He pulled me in tight.

"Your mom would have made me see how important he is, that we have to keep him."

I lay back on the pillows, saw my dad was there with me, saw him listening while I talked.

And he told me about Jed, the story Jed had told him when I went to find Sam. A long story of searching people's eyes, people's faces, for the home he had to find, for the promise he had made.

"Jed said that while he had him, the dog protected him from a gang, frightened the life out of them." He smiled. "That doesn't surprise me," he said, "great monster of a thing he's grown into."

We both laughed, because he didn't mean monster at all.

He looked into my eyes. "It was the dog that found you and Sam at the lake. I just followed him."

Dad rested his head on mine.

"I was so . . . I hadn't noticed you'd gone."

I could see something in his eyes, like he was remembering something important deep in his heart.

"Dad?"

It took him a minute to look up.

"Say it again," he said. "I've missed you saying Dad."

"Please, Dad, he belongs with us."

"I see that too," he said. "Has he got a name?"

"Homeless," I said.

Dad laughed.

"We'll have to think of a new one."

❧ Forty-Three ❧

Sam was lying in his hospital bed, with plastic tubes and wires all around him, machines beeping.

Mrs. Cooper hugged me. "Talk to Sam," she said. "He's feeling weak, but I know he'd like to hear you're all right."

Sam was pale; his lips were dark. His eyes opened and rolled a little as I touched his hand.

"It's me, Cally," I spelled.

He waved into the air as if he knew that Dad was standing there. His hand was feeble, but he spelled out, "Are you talking now?"

"Yes," I said.

Mrs. Cooper looked at Dad, and they smiled at each other.

"*Yes!*" I shouted.

"I can hear you," said Sam.

❧Forty-Four❧

I stayed home from school all week with Dad. We rearranged the furniture, squeezed everything in, including Homeless, painted my bedroom walls forget-me-not blue, the ceiling too. Homeless stuck by my side, put his nose in my boxes when I emptied them, watched all the things find new homes in my room. When Dad watched TV, he'd lie on Dad's feet, keep him company. I saw Dad looking at Homeless, saw Dad wonder at him. How big he was, how brave he was, how he had managed to tell us everything about himself.

We visited Sam in the hospital all week, and he got stronger, but he needed special care. He had a heart murmur. It made me wonder what brilliant and extraordinary things it murmured to him. The doctors said Sam would still need to have his operation, maybe a new heart. I didn't think there was a heart in the world to replace the one he had. But for now they were going to give him some new medicine and some more tests until he was stronger.

When Sam was allowed home, we left all the doors open inside 4 Albert Terrace, let Homeless move about among us. And I will take Sam swimming one day. We'll find a way.

"It's me, Grandma. It's Cally."

Grandma went quiet when I answered the phone.

"You sounded just like—" Then she said, "I'm glad to hear your voice, sweetheart."

I knew who she meant I sounded like. But she didn't say very much, just asked how we were settling into our new apartment and if we were all well. Grandpa took the phone then, saying Grandma needed a little sit-down and that they'd come visit soon.

Luke, as always, had his back facing his bedroom door, his eyes on his computer. But the door was open. He swiveled around because he knew I was there with Homeless. He ruffled his head, made Homeless's tail swing.

"I like having him here. Sort of makes it feel more like home."

"Do you think he should have a new name?"

"Nah, it's not his name that's important."

"We've got the end-of-term concert tonight," I said. "You coming?"

"You going to sing?"

"If they'll let me."

"Course they will. And we're all coming, aren't we, boy?"

I leaned over the back of Luke's chair and rested my chin on his shoulder. Homeless rested his head on Luke's lap and watched, as if he were part of everything going on. I saw Luke had photos of all of us stuck around his computer. And a big one of Rachel.

"What are you going to sing? I'll find the words for you."

He looked up the words on the computer and

wrote them down for me.

There was a gentle knock at the front door. Homeless padded out.

"I'll get it," called Dad.

After a moment Dad came into Luke's room.

"There's somebody to see you, Cally," he said.

Homeless was standing next to Jed. Jed had new clothes that fitted him, a nice jacket. His eyes crinkled and twinkled; his dimples were pressed deep in his cheeks.

"Thank you for Homeless," I said. "Thank you for bringing him home."

He chuckled.

"I never heard you speak before," he said. "Lovely eyes, lovely voice." His voice was gentle. "Just like your mom."

And we stood for a minute without saying anything. I suppose it had all been said.

"I got a job," he said, "at The Music Shop."

He looked so pleased with himself. I just felt like bursting with happiness for him.

"Good for you," said Dad, standing back, holding out his arm for Jed to come in.

"Come to the concert tonight," I said, holding his

hands. "I'm going to sing. Honestly, I sing pretty good, don't I, Dad?"

"Like a bird," he said. "Like your mom."

Jed smiled. And so did Dad.

Then Jed said, "There was something else."

He reached into his pocket. He had a small blue cardboard box, about the same size as a matchbox, worn on the corners, tied with a crushed ribbon. He handed it to Dad.

"For me?" Dad said, confused.

Dad opened the box.

"She said to tell you happy birthday."

Inside the box was a new pick for his guitar. It was silver and inscribed with tiny words: *Love always, Louise.*

❧ Forty-Five ❧

Mr. Crisp was on the stage in the assembly hall. A red pencil behind his ear stuck through his misty hair. Song sheets and music books were scattered over his piano.

I held out Luke's paper for him.

"Can I sing this one?"

He looked at the paper, at the song I was going to sing called "If There's a Star."

"It's the song from *Olivia!* where she gets sent to sing in town, where she sings for all the people, brings them all together."

"So you'll get to sing as Olivia after all," he said, beaming. "I think I've still got the music from last year somewhere."

He went over to his piano and started rummaging in his piano seat.

"In that case, you need to go practice some scales, get those vocals cords warmed and stretched."

He took a deep breath, and his belly filled in his hands.

"Do you remember what I said about your breathing?"

I nodded.

"Remember, feel that breath fill your belly, push against your ribs. Remember your breathing; it carries the song."

"I know," I said. "Sounds end up coming out of your mouth, but they start much, much farther down."

He laughed, a great big lovely laugh.

"Shoo!" he said. "Go practice. I need to get some practice in myself. Make her proud, make us all proud," he called.

Harry Turner is the best boy singer in the school. His dad played a harmonica while he sang his song for everyone. Mr. Turner winked at me when it was my turn, put another music book on the music stand, and left the stage. Dad came onstage and sat on the chair. He had his guitar and silver plectrum.

"Ready?" he said.

I saw into his loving eyes. He looked at me like I was everything.

This was the last time I saw my mom in the world. She didn't have her raincoat and hat. She was standing by the side of the stage. She whispered, *I just wanted to hear you sing once more.* Luke stood at the back with Rachel, Jed, and Homeless, who was quiet because he had all his family nearby. Mrs. Cooper and Sam had front seats, and Sam was holding one of his cards. It said GIFT.

I would have sung this last year in the school musical of *Olivia!* Mom didn't get to hear me back then, but I knew she was listening now.

Read on for the first few chapters of
Sarah Lean's next novel, *A Hundred Horses*

❧ One ❧

Mom was late picking me up from drama club again. Which meant another twenty minutes of not wanting to be there. There was just me looking through the window as all the other children left. I had one more thing to avoid, and then I could forget what happened earlier.

Me and this boy named Jamie were extras and scenery painters, doing background colors, which was just about all right with us, if we had to be there at all. So I thought if anyone was on my side, it would be Jamie. But he wasn't. Especially not when he told Mrs. Oliver that I was out back doing dangerous things with the wiring.

Mrs. Oliver blew a fuse and said I should explain myself. I looked at her and took a breath and was about to speak, but then I didn't know what "explaining myself" meant. You can't explain yourself. You're just you. Even though what actually happened wasn't like me at all. I'd never, ever done anything like that before.

The heat in my face made my eyes sting because I was suddenly thinking about what Mom would say.

"Well?" Mrs. Oliver folded her arms.

"Well, what happened was this," I said, deciding to tell her the events like a story. "I finished doing the scenery painting, like you said, and Jamie and me had washed the brushes and we were just leaving them to dry and I found those lights . . . you know—the ones you were looking for? And they were in a bag with other things that needed fixing and the plug was missing and I knew how to join them to another set of lights. So I just did it, but I forgot to ask and . . . I didn't mean to do it."

"Nell Green, this is so unlike you," she said. "What were you thinking, playing with such dangerous things?"

Which was silly because it wasn't dangerous; the

lights weren't even plugged in, so nothing bad was going to happen. And maybe that made me look as if I wasn't sorry enough.

So I said, "Sorry, Mrs. Oliver, I won't do it again."

Mainly I was thinking, Please don't tell Mom. Which made my face blush and prickle again.

"Who knows what might have happened?" Mrs. Oliver said. "What would your mother say?"

Sometimes you wish people could read your mind.

It didn't seem to matter that there was now an extralong string of lights for the scenery. Mrs. Oliver didn't expect an answer, though, because she turned on her heel and clomped across the wooden floor.

So there I was with my face pushed against the window, looking as far down the road as I could to watch out for Mom's car, hoping Mrs. Oliver wouldn't see her arrive. But she did, and they discussed the incident through the car window. Now it was an *incident*, like some great big disaster.

I was belted in my seat, sandwiched between their conversation. Mrs. Oliver said what an unusual skill I had, but that I should be discouraged from messing with electrical things. Surely she meant fixing! Mom agreed instantly and gave me a look that said, How could you?, which was what I mostly wanted to avoid. That look.

"Maybe Nell needs more to do," Mom said. "Something more challenging to keep her occupied, Mrs. Oliver. A bigger part in the play perhaps?"

One little thing was now turning into a major drama.

Keep quiet, I told myself. Starting Monday there'll be two weeks of spring vacation with Nana. Mom will be too busy with work and a conference, so there'll be no after-school clubs, no appointments, no waiting. Just me and Nana relaxing at her house, watching daytime TV, playing cards and computer bingo, safe and quiet. Nana doesn't drive and she won't take the bus because you never know who's sat on the seat before you or where they've been, so she can't take me to rehearsals. Ha! And Mrs. Oliver was bound to forget.

Mom drove away, saying, "Do we need to have a talk?"

"No," I said. Because her betrayed face said everything.

❦Two❦

Waiting again. This time in the car while Mom rushed into the supermarket on the way home. She didn't leave the keys behind, so I couldn't open the windows or listen to the radio. I could only hear something rumbling outside and my own sighing.

Waiting makes you sigh. And sighing makes a white patch on the window so you can write "hello" backward.

An old lady with a shopping cart stopped to read my message. So I smiled. But she frowned and walked on. So I wiped the window and watched a giant, thundering yellow crane instead. It turned slowly in the sky, with a big chunk of concrete swinging on a thin wire below it. I didn't blink for ages, just watching it sway.

Mom came out of the supermarket, shopping bags in both hands, her big black handbag, containing everything anyone could possibly need (and probably a hundred more things as well), weighing down her shoulder. Her phone was crushed between the strap and her ear.

I watch her face for clues and can usually work things out and guess what she's decided. She has an are-you-listening-carefully face, a don't-question-me-I-know-what-I'm-doing face, and a slightly smiley making-up-for-what's-missing face the rest of the time. And I could tell two things by the way her eyes were fixed on me as she walked and talked. The two things I could tell were this: first, the phone call was about me, and second, I didn't have a choice.

"There's been a change of plan," Mom said, swinging the shopping bags into the backseat. "You're going to Aunt Liv's for your vacation."

I wasn't expecting that.

"But I always stay with Nana. Why have you changed it? Because I touched those stupid lights?"

Whatever she was about to say, she didn't.

"It has nothing to do with that."

"Yes, it has. You've changed it because of what happened earlier."

"That's not it at all. Nana's had to go up to Leicester on the train to look after her cousin who's fallen. Auntie Annabel. You remember her?"

Nope. And if you fold your arms, you don't have to try to remember either.

"The one with the poodle," Mom said, and I could hear her trying hard not to make this about the incident.

I couldn't picture Auntie Annabel, just a trembling pinkish poodle and a funny smell of ham.

"I thought you said it died."

"Yes, but you know who I mean."

"Why can't somebody else look after her? Why does it have to be Nana?"

Mom continued as if I'd said nothing.

"The decision's been made. When we get home, I want you to go up to the attic. There's a big gray suitcase up there that you're going to need."

I noticed we'd completely left out a whole middle bit of the conversation where I could say I don't want to go. Which is always part of Mom's master plan. Cut out the annoying middle bit and get to the point, or the next appointment. Never mind what I want.

"Start packing tonight," she said. "You can do the rest tomorrow when we get back from your math tutor and before swimming club; then I'll drive you down to Aunt Liv's on Sunday."

I don't like drama club, and I don't like the math tutor either because her house smells like garlic. My swimming teacher says I swim like a cat, like something that doesn't want to be in the water.

My life is a list of mostly boring or pointless activities that I didn't choose, with a car drive and waiting in between. If you practice long enough, you don't have to care that everything has been taken out of your hands. That's what moms are for.

"So how was drama club? Apart from—"

"Fine." I sighed.

When we got home, we ate cold pasta salad out of supermarket cartons. Mom had her phone glued to her head again, and while she was talking, she waved a finger toward the attic door in the hallway ceiling at the top of the stairs.

❧ Three ❧

O ur attic was as silent as the moon. Except for my footsteps, which sounded hollow against the boards. The yellow padding in the sloping walls blocked out the sounds of the world. It felt like a place from long ago that had stopped, with its old air and old things we keep because they don't belong at the dump or in a thrift shop or anywhere else but with us.

I saw the gray suitcase. And I could have just grabbed it and gone straight back downstairs. Instead, I pushed my shoulders back and turned my chin up. I was going to make a stand. And I didn't mind being up there where the world had paused and nobody could see me or hear me. Just a few minutes of pretending . . .

I imagined telling Mom what I really thought.

Now listen, Mother, I don't want to go to any stupid clubs. You see, I don't like them, and I don't really have any friends at them because I'm not very good at anything and I'm not interested either. Now you want to dump me in a place where I don't know anyone and I'll have to do a whole load more things that I don't care about. And I know how much it upset you and reminded you of Dad, even though you didn't say . . . but I did actually want to fix those lights. And I really liked doing it.

I didn't mean to think that last bit. And I knew I'd never be brave enough to say any of those things.

I sat down in the old dust and sighed. That's when I noticed the tidy pile of cardboard boxes that I was sitting next to. I decided to open the top one.

Inside there was an old Mother's Day card with crushed tissue flowers on the front and a lined notebook with big, uncertain handwriting and pages and pages of scratchy drawings of a house with five-legged animals in it. At the bottom of the box were clumpy clay models and strange mixed-up creatures made from cardboard, wires, and feathers and buttons. An elephant-giraffe with a long neck and a trunk, a hippo-bird with two clawed legs, and other impossible animals. It's funny how you can't remember making these things, even though you must be the same person with the same hands.

I noticed then that the cardboard box had a sticker on it. It said NELL—AGE FOUR. All the boxes had stickers saying my name and my age. Year by year, everything I'd made had been stored in a pile, getting taller every year. I looked inside some more of them. All the other boxes had schoolbooks and reports in them. How come I didn't make things anymore?

That's when I saw a brown leather suitcase behind the boxes, lying alone in the shadows under the eaves, forgotten under dust. It was a bit bigger than my school backpack and quite heavy. I heard things shifting inside as I dragged it over by the handle. The leather was worn, the seams grazed, like skin protecting the tender things inside.

There was no sticker on it with my name, but I flicked the latches open anyway.

Inside was like an ancient tomb, full of flat pieces

of metal with holes around the edges, narrow strips like silver bones, scattered among ornaments and precious objects. I rummaged through the pieces and found a musical box and sixteen miniature painted horses. I liked the way one fitted in my hand with my fingers under its metal belly and its neck against my thumb. Its galloping legs were frozen in time, its silent eyes wide open. And then I remembered what it was.

Once all the pieces had made a mechanical carousel, almost as big as our coffee table, but taller. I was four when I last saw the brilliance of it, when I last saw the lights and spinning horses. I opened the lined notebook again, the one from when I was four. That's what the pictures were! Not strange creatures with five legs, but horses with long tails, and they weren't in a house, they were on a carousel. And then I remembered the buzzing in my skin and brain, the laugh alive in my tummy as I had crouched and gazed at the swirling, whirling carousel.

I held the strings of tiny lights. I could see the filaments inside, as fine as baby hair. I arranged the horses in a circle. I poked the wires from the lights into a black battery cylinder. My hands remembered what to do. The lights burned, white and gold and pink. I turned the handle on the musical box, heard the rusty chimes speed up and come to life. All the fragments lay around me, all the pieces. But I thought the horses kicked; I thought they were spinning beside me, as if they were alive.

"Nell? Can't you find it?" Mom called. "Do you need me to come up and look?"

I scrambled to scoop all the pieces back up, to hide them away again.

"No! Don't come up!" I said quickly as I snapped the suitcase shut. "I've found it."

Then I wondered what would be in a box called NELL—AGE ELEVEN. And I remembered why I didn't make things anymore.

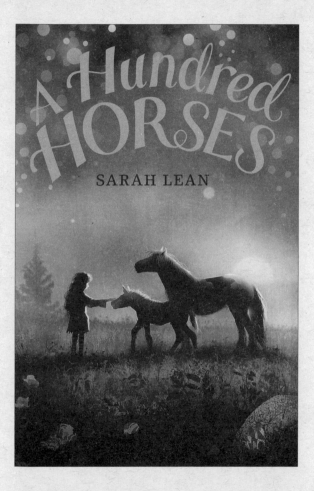